Poet to Poet
Tennyson Selected b

D0293046

ALFRED, LORD TENNYSON was born in 1809 at
Somersby, Lincolnshire, the sixth of twelve children of a
clergyman. He went up to Cambridge (1828–31) but did
not obtain a degree. He never had any other occupation
than poet. In 1845 he was granted a state pension of
£200 a year (in today's terms about £2,500 after tax),
and in 1850 Tennyson was created Poet Laureate. He
accepted a peerage in 1883. After a short illness he died
in 1892 and was buried in Westminster Abbey.

KINGSLEY AMIS was born in 1922 and was educated at
the City of London School and St John's College,
Oxford. Apart from many novels he has published three
volumes of poems, *A Frame of Mind* (1953), *A Case of
Samples* (1956), *A Look Round the Estate* (1967), and a
selection of his poems is included in *Penguin Modern
Poets* 2. Some of his best known novels are *Lucky Jim,
Take a Girl Like You, That Uncertain Feeling* (all three
have been made into films, the last-named entitled *Only
Two Can Play*), *The Green Man*, and his latest
publication, *Girl, 20*.

TENNYSON

Selected by

Kingsley Amis

Penguin Books

Penguin Books Ltd, Harmondsworth,
Middlesex, England
Penguin Books Inc., 7110 Ambassador Road,
Baltimore, Maryland 21207, U.S.A.
Penguin Books Australia Ltd, Ringwood,
Victoria, Australia

First published 1973
Selection copyright © Penguin Books Ltd, 1973
Introduction copyright © Kingsley Amis, 1973

Made and printed in Great Britain by
Richard Clay (The Chaucer Press) Ltd
Bungay, Suffolk
Set in Monotype Ehrhardt

Contents

Introduction

It is not very much longer than ten years ago that Tennyson's poetry began to regain the kind of serious attention and acclaim it had begun to lose a century earlier, when the poet still had thirty years to live: surely a record length of time for any comparatively modern artist to spend in the wilderness. T. S. Eliot published in 1936 an eloquent defence that remains the best short account of Tennyson's genius; W. H. Auden brought out a selection of the verse, with some helpful and provocative introductory remarks, in 1946; but these, along with a few lesser names, made little lasting impression on what had become a massive prejudice.

There are perhaps three main reasons for this history of neglect – a neglect at or near the top, we should notice, rather than among the wider poetry-reading public, who have always seen to it that Tennyson's works remained very much in print. The first reason is that, from a distance, he can look just like an incarnation of Victorianism, pompous, unthinkingly patriotic, Poet Laureate (a crime by definition), the dutiful voice of the hierarchical system of that day, the bedside reading of Prince Albert and the Queen herself. None of Tennyson's best poems are vulnerable to this sort of charge, but it was the basis of a large and lasting reaction against him among people to whom the kind of society he seemed to stand for had produced the First World War and its aftermath.

Secondly, and more recently, his verse has turned out to be resistant to modern techniques of literary criticism. It holds no interesting ambiguities, intentional or unintentional; there are no puzzles, no 'levels of meaning' within it; it just is. All the critic can say about most of it comes down to, 'Look at this. Good (or bad), isn't it?' This is as much as a great deal of what passes for criticism is really saying, but with other poets – Donne, for instance, that notable purveyor of mere complication – it is easier to seem to be saying more. Tennyson eludes such attempts. His symbolism, moreover, is plain and transparent, and, as Auden remarked, 'no other poetry is easier, and less illuminating, to psycho-analyse'.

The third factor that has told against Tennyson's repute is more difficult to dismiss, if not impossible. A reading of his early verse, that written by the time he was twenty-one, say, shows him to have been possessed of stupendous inborn gifts, a child of the Muses who makes the Keats of that age look all fingers and thumbs. We should have to go back to Milton (whom Tennyson greatly admired) to find an English poet of comparable natural endowment, or, since Milton's early efforts smell of ink as well as inspiration, it might be more instructive to go outside literature altogether and invoke the youthful Mozart. Like the composer, Tennyson grew into and remained a quite uninteresting man, though, again like him, he was a very interesting phenomenon: a genius. But Mozart made only the most temporary compromises with the demands of his gift, whereas Tennyson deliberately threw his away, to become in time a figure uncomfortably close to that pensioner of the establishment taken by many in the past to be all he had ever been. So, at any rate, I would argue, as the latest of a thin but unbroken line of commentators beginning a good hundred years ago. The story really starts, however, earlier still, when Tennyson's first books appeared in the 1820s and early '30s.

Their critical reception was largely hostile, and the nature of that hostility is significant. Some of it was directed at supposed technical flaws: Coleridge recommended a course in versification, a piece of advice that seems little short of absurd today. What was bothering him and others might have been the spectacle of so young a newcomer (two complete volumes and a large contribution to a third by the age of twenty-three) not only very much at home in any established poetic form, but able to invent fresh ones in which he moved with equal facility. This line of attack we can discount, though Tennyson did not, as we shall see. Far more telling were accusations of a lack of intellectual and moral content. Here, to all appearance, was another Romantic poet, and England had had, or should have had, enough of them.

It was clearly felt, if never openly stated, that a new and potentially great poet – even the sternest detractors saw that – must not be self-indulgent and perhaps sensual like Keats, nor an irresponsible atheist like Shelley, nor a republican and a debauchee like Byron. (All three, having died in the half dozen years before Tennyson's first appearance, were fresh in the public mind.) No, such a man must be staid and pious like Southey or Wordsworth – respectively the current and succeeding Poets Laureate. Victorian in the grimmer sense before Victoria was on the throne, such critics condemned in Tennyson an 'unbounded indulgence in the mere luxuries of poetry', a failure to 'instruct', an ignorance of the vital fact that 'true poetry must benefit humanity'. John Stuart Mill, in an otherwise friendly article, told Tennyson that he must cultivate philosophy as well as poetry; a few years later, Monckton Milnes informed him that 'the function of the poet in this day of ours is to teach still more than he delights' – this from a man who was to become notorious as the owner of the largest collection of pornography in Victorian London.

Tennyson was sensitive to criticism. Nearly all artists are, major and minimal alike; Shakespeare surely was not, but we should run a mile rather than generalize from him. Milton never forgave a slight; Virgil, another hero of Tennyson's, would certainly have behaved in the same way, had the practice of reviewing flourished in classical Rome; it was impossible to converse with Beethoven except on the basis that he was the greatest composer who had ever lived. None of these three, however, would have swerved an inch from the course he had set himself if God had given him a hostile notice. Tennyson was made of less stern stuff. He minded adverse criticism in a double sense: he was stung by it, and he took notice of it. He introduced technical revisions, arguably for the better, in the directions suggested to him; he also, and disastrously, went against his nature by abandoning the luxuries of poetry, cultivating philosophy, and trying to teach more than he delighted. To give Pope's line a different bearing from that intended, he progressively 'stooped to truth, and moralized his song'.

One man really understood and appreciated the true nature of Tennyson's gift: Arthur H. Hallam, whom he met at Cambridge in 1829 and who soon became the closest friend of his life. In an article which would have been outstandingly acute whoever had written it, let alone somebody of twenty, Hallam drew a distinction between the poetry of reflection, exemplified in Wordsworth, and the poetry of sensation (or feeling), as seen in the work of Keats, Shelley and Tennyson. Hallam argued a preference for the second category on the grounds of its superior immediacy and beauty; we need not agree with him on that point in order to see at once that he had placed Tennyson where he belonged. Of the two friends, Hallam, though a year and a half the younger, was the dominating partner and certainly the more intelligent. Had he remained on the scene, he might well have lent Tennyson the support to continue along the path of lyrical expression for which nature had designed him.* But all too soon Hallam,

---

* 'Whenever the mind of the artist suffers itself to be occupied, during its periods of creation, by any other predominant motive than the desire of beauty, the result is false in art' – not Oscar Wilde, not Walter Pater, not D. G. Rossetti, but Hallam in the article referred to. That he was able to forecast so early the direction English poetry was to take in the second

away on a trip to Vienna, was dead of a brain haemorrhage at the age of twenty-two.

The loss of Hallam was, obviously enough, the crucial event in Tennyson's emotional life, and its reverberations can be felt in his work until the end. It is equally plain that he had loved the dead man, often falling into the language of love in writing about him; but we had better be clear in our mind that, as certainly as can be in such matters, there was nothing physical in their relationship. The importance to us of that loss is that it made Tennyson into a great poet, in one sense despite himself and his attempts to alter the direction of his development, in another sense inevitably. For his whole poetic nature was made to express loss and the feelings that lie close to it: despondency, ennui, nostalgia, loneliness, despair and the desire for reconciliation and resignation.

So much is clear from poems of his that antedate Hallam's death, notably 'Mariana' and 'Œnone', while, in a less specific way, 'A spirit haunts' reads like a forecast of grief. 'Mariana' is a very easy poem to like, and, what is rarer, to like for the right reasons. It embodies to perfection that characteristically Tennysonian power which generations of critics have tried to define, but none more successfully than the unknown contributor to *Tait's Edinburgh Magazine* for August, 1842, who praised Tennyson's 'power of making the picturesque delineation of external nature illustrate the mood of mind portrayed'. (At that time, 'picturesque' retained its original meaning of 'pictorial, in the style of a picture' and had not yet degenerated into a vague journalistic synonym for 'odd' or 'intriguing'. 'Sharply visual' would be a rough modern equivalent – but nobody could miss the tremendous aural effects of 'Mariana'.)

'Œnone' embodies the same theme in a totally different

---

half of the century is an impressive feat. He was also, however, making a terribly accurate unconscious prophecy about what was going to happen to the poetry of Tennyson.

style. The tune, too, is different: blank verse that sounds as if nobody else had ever used the form, an achievement in itself for a young poet who had Milton looking over his shoulder and Wordsworth, so to speak, at the next writing-table. Here, twice at least, Tennyson brings the inner and outer worlds, mind and nature, to the point of coalescence. Œnone's memory of Paris's kisses can hardly be distinguished from the present reality, in her eyes and ears, of the whirling river, and, a little later, the loudness of the stream and the trembling of the stars are not only things experienced but also the prelude or accompaniment to a hysterical swoon.

'The Lotos-Eaters' deals in similar ways with another aspect of melancholy, definable as languor, about which it manages to become energetic, ending indeed in a kind of rocket-burst of lassitude and capitulation. 'Ulysses', Tennyson's first important poem after the news of Hallam's death reached him, is a much less straightforward affair. It looks like a downright, almost artless call to action, a pre-Victorian exaltation of the heroic virtues and correspondingly an attack on loafing. Tennyson himself said, 'it was written under the sense of loss and that all had gone by, but that still life must be fought out to the end'. Well, he should know. Yet all sorts of critics have felt that the piece is not quite doing what it claims to be doing. As early as 1855, the historian Goldwin Smith wrote of 'the Homeric Ulysses, the man of purpose and action' shown by Tennyson as roaming aimlessly, 'merely to relieve his ennui, and dragging his companions with him. We should rather say, he intends to roam, but stands for ever a listless and melancholy figure on the shore.'

Smith connected Ulysses's deficiency of genuine vigour with what he saw as Tennyson's overall inability to paint 'the active life with real zest' – a sound observation, if not as damaging as Smith evidently thought. Another view, well argued by E. J. Chiasson, is that the poem is doing the exact opposite of what it seems to claim to be doing, and is actually an attack on irresponsibility,* like 'The Lotos-Eaters'. At least two points strongly support Chiasson's reading: the hypocrisy which leads Ulysses to praise Telemachus for qualities which, as the opening lines show, he himself has no time for; and the 'jovial agnosticism' with which he considers the expedition's eventual fate – it may be this, it may be that, and the verse at that stage does seem to carry a bored shrug of the shoulders. What weighs against this interpretation, apart from Tennyson's statement, is the squaring of the shoulders that at once follows the shrug and ends the poem on a note of conviction and nobility, a rather self-conscious nobility, perhaps, but noble all the same. Let the reader decide, or decide he need not decide.

There are no mysteries about 'Morte d'Arthur', to the subject of which Tennyson may have been immediately drawn by the coincidence of Hallam's Christian name, though he had long been interested in the Arthurian myths. The pictorial passages are splendid, and the musical ones too, notably the final journey to the lake and the violent change of key on arrival there. Nevertheless, all is not well. There are contrived austerities of diction and syntax, the earliest signs of the rift within the lute – Tennyson's own phrase in a different context. He was not yet cultivating philosophy very assiduously, but he was casting a colder eye on the luxuries of poetry. When we read 'Morte d'Arthur' as incorporated virtually unchanged in *The Idylls of the King* (published in instalments 1859–85), it does not stand out from the arid wastes of that ersatz epic as boldly as we should like.

For a dozen years after the original poem was written, roughly 1834–45, Tennyson's development followed a winding course. He was already at work on what was to become *In*

---

*Auden, seeing the same things in the poem as Chiasson, but interpreting them differently, had asked, 'What is "Ulysses" but a covert – the weakness of the poem is its indirection – refusal to be a responsible and useful person, a glorification of the heroic dandy?'

Memoriam, but with no clear intention of ever publishing it. Much of what he wrote he considered unworthy of inclusion in his final collected edition. He was casting about, trying lighter verse ('Will Waterproof's Lyrical Monologue'), trying, with untoward results, to ape Wordsworth, occasionally recalling his earlier lyrical simplicities ('Break, break, break' – Hallam again – or 'Come not, when I am dead'), once or twice successfully shaping something new ('Locksley Hall' – successful against all the odds). Then, at the end of this period, he did what a large section of opinion had been telling him to do and got down to a long poem that would teach moral lessons, show human sympathy, and concern itself with questions of the day.

The result was *The Princess*, and most, though not quite all, of it is a hard read. He had attempted to tell a story, and he could not tell a story; to create character, and he could not create character; to be dramatic, and he was no good at that either. All that is of value, and it is very valuable, is the lyrics he smuggled into the narrative. Some of these went under the camouflage of being in blank verse, like the main body of the poem, and at least two of them are among the finest things he ever wrote. 'Tears, idle tears' (Hallam again) is probably the most poignant cry of despair in the language, and refutes by itself any notion that Tennyson was nothing but a complacent Victorian. (Some recent critics have tried to implant difficulties in it; these shrink as soon as we see that 'idle' means not worthless or trifling, but useless, vain.) 'Come down, O maid' is a sustained flight of the purely lyrical, a vehicle of excitement and exultation unique in Tennyson, a sound-piece again unique in English. The rhymed songs he infiltrated in the 1850 edition of the poem are less fine, but still fine; indeed, yet again it is hard to think of anything in mere words that suggests actual music more strongly than 'Sweet and low'.

1850 was the pivotal year in Tennyson's life. Very nearly

all his best, even his good, poetry was already written; it could be argued that most of very nearly all had been written by 1843, and a lot of that most by 1834. More specifically, in May of 1850 he published his greatest work, *In Memoriam A.H.H.*, after sixteen years' preparation; in the June he got married, after twelve years' delay; in November he was appointed Poet Laureate, after seven months' interregnum since the death of Wordsworth. One event of that year, taking place on its first day, he most likely did not notice: the appearance of a new magazine, *The Germ*, the organ of the Pre-Raphaelite Brotherhood. This curious body, though mainly concerned with the visual arts, and though intermittently dogged by what we should now call social-realist convictions, had rediscovered Hallam's notion that the prime duty of art was to be beautiful, not moral, not useful, not acceptable. The PRB and their disciples could have formed Tennyson's ideal audience, could have encouraged him to remake himself as a lyric poet, had they cared to do so. But, even if they had, it would have been too late. He was set on his course, for the remaining forty-two years of his life, as the Christian, humanitarian, democratic poet of official Victorianism.

The greatness of *In Memoriam* starts from the fact that, in it, Tennyson had as if by chance come across the form that perfectly reconciled his gifts, his destined subject-matter and his aspirations. It is a long poem that is not a long poem at all, but a series of lyrics loosely connected by continuity or change of mood, without narrative, characters or dramatization. Rather as the tension of *Paradise Lost* springs from Milton's quarrel with himself about the difficulty yet necessity of justifying the ways of God to men, so Tennyson is torn between despairing grief and the need and duty to resist it. He called *In Memoriam* 'rather the cry of the whole human race than mine'; it is both; for once, but what a once, he spoke for his fellow-man *without having set out to do so*. Eliot's splendid essay calls it 'a poem of despair, but of despair of a religious kind' (adding, no less truly, that its author was 'the most instinctive rebel against the society in which he was the most perfect conformist'). Ostensibly, the poem comes out for faith and optimism; really and poetically, despair carries the day. To feel this, we need look no further than the contrast in conviction between sections CVI and CVII (the first half of the latter), but it is at the heart of the whole, so that even the most unfelt assertions of eternal Providence carry the pathos of a whistling in the dark.

It remains to try to justify the assertion that Tennyson's gift had effectively perished by 1850, if not at some rather or considerably earlier date. The merits of *In Memoriam* might seem to refute the more extravagant versions of such a charge, but we know that at least half of the poem was already drafted by 1842, and we can fairly safely assume – at any rate I would strongly suspect – that a good deal more than that was there then. Other apparent exceptions to the suggested rule tend to disappear on investigation, or at least to become fuzzy. 'Tithonus' was first published in 1860, but 'Tithon', written in 1833 and not disinterred until 1949, provides a good four-fifths of the official version. It may show lack of taste to erect any kind of question-mark alongside 'Crossing the Bar', undeniably written in 1889 and a genuine and touching poem; all the same, we may doubt whether Tennyson at his best would have let pass the minor but distracting enigmas in the first and last stanzas (see Notes).

'Milton' (1863) is a more interesting, not to say fascinating, case in point. It is not only a magnificent piece, deeply romantic and Romantic, unashamedly lyrical and stuffed with the luxuries of poetry; it is also, in its conclusion, shamelessly personal, unedifying, unmoral, exotic and pagan – all qualities the Laureate was pledged to abjure. Or rather, it was not shamelessly, not openly, any of that; Tennyson smuggled it in, in the manner of the *Princess* lyrics, as an experiment in the use of Latin metres in English. The result is a technical feat unequalled in our language (one of the things that marks Tennyson as a great poet is the tally of his uniquenesses) in that 'Milton' makes metrical sense in English while adhering strictly to the utterly alien prescriptions of the Latin form – a feat appreciable only by those disappearing few who know Latin. But, of course, the point of this performance is that it gave Tennyson sanction to say what he would not have dared to say in his natural voice.

The 'Epigrams' were never printed in any form in his lifetime. They reveal not only the sensitivity to criticism already described, but something less predictable, a spiteful humour and vulgarity that was very much part of the man, though its chief outlet was in remarks to friends and others and recorded only in their memoirs. He wrote a pompous, but as always competent, ode that was set to music by Sterndale Bennett and sung by a choir of thousands at the opening of the International Exhibition in 1862; on a visit there he is supposed to have peevishly asked a companion, 'Is there anywhere in this damned place where we can get a decent bottle of Bass?' The gap thus revealed between two aspects of Tennyson is dismayingly as well as comically wide. The Bass-seeking Tennyson could never have hoped to find a hearing in Victorian England, unless under a pseudonym, and that suppression weakens the Tennyson we have.

W. H. Auden has drawn attention to the difficulty facing any lyric poet, that of finding work to do in the long and frequent intervals between his necessarily brief bursts of activity. Such a poet finds no difficulty today: he writes fiction, journalism, even advertising copy. But in the nineteenth century, and above all for a Poet Laureate, this kind of solution was not available; a poet was expected to be a poet all the time. Just as many of us would give large parts of Keats ('The Cap and Bells', for instance) for a few short stories by him, large parts of Browning (*Sordello*, for instance) for a travel book, etc., so I at least would give very large parts of

Tennyson, from *The Princess* onwards, for some of the down-to-earth comic poetry he had it in him to write. In that medium he might have become the true commentator on those old 'questions of the day' he grievously failed to be.

As I have said, the view that Tennyson in some sense yielded to critical and social pressure, unmade his genius by an act of will, is far from being a new one. The reaction against him did not begin in the 1920s. Lewis Carroll produced a cruel and very funny parody of one of his styles in 1856, Swinburne another such in 1880. An acute French observer, the critic Hippolyte Taine, wrote of Tennyson in 1864:

He has chosen his ideas, chiselled his words, equalled by his artifices, felicities, and diversities of style, the pleasantness and perfection of social elegance in the midst of which we read him . . . [His poetry] seems made expressly for these wealthy, cultivated, leisured business men, heirs of the ancient nobility, new leaders of a new England. It is part of their luxury as of their morality; it is an eloquent confirmation of their principles, and a precious article of their drawing-room furniture.

And Alfred Austin, a third-rate poet who, by a sort of irony, became Laureate in 1896, wrote in 1870 a curmudgeonly and envious article which nevertheless contained the inescapable truth that Tennyson's 'fame has increased precisely as his genuine poetical power has steadily waned'.

If he has never been short of detractors, Tennyson has had his defenders too, not least on the matter in hand. A modern critic, W. W. Robson, argues effectively against the view that Tennyson 'made himself express the attitudes of his age to large public subjects not because he really wanted to do this or was capable of it but because he felt he ought to'. But that is not quite the issue. No doubt he did feel he ought to, but what he felt more strongly was that he would have to if he was going to be what he had always set his mind on becoming, the poet of his age. Early in life he told one of his brothers, 'I mean to be famous.' And, although in most respects a very unworldly man, he was astute enough, or intuitive enough, to see how to be famous in the England of his day.

That England notoriously had its doubts as well as its certainties, its neuroses as well as its moral health, its fits of gloom and frustration and panic as well as its complacency. Tennyson is the voice of those doubts and their accompaniments, and his genius enabled him to communicate them in such a way that we can understand them and feel them as our own. In short, we know from experience just what he means. Eliot called him the saddest of all English poets, and I cannot improve on that judgement. Tennyson spoke for everybody in a sense he never consciously intended – not everybody all the time, in any mood, but everybody at some time or other, when the whole world seems to have gone wrong. He was the deeply unofficial, small-letter poet laureate of that feeling.

KINGSLEY AMIS

Sources

The texts of this selection are those of the monumental and indispensable *Tennyson*, edited by Christopher Ricks, in the Longman series of Annotated English Poets, from which I have also taken a great deal of information. In addition, I am indebted to *Tennyson: an introduction and a selection* by W. H. Auden (Phoenix House); *Tennyson: the growth of a poet* by J. H. Buckley and *Tennyson and the Reviewers* by E. F. Shannon Jr (both Harvard University Press); *Critical Essays on the Poetry of Tennyson* edited by E. J. Kilham and *Tennyson: the critical heritage* edited by J. D. Jump (both Routledge); and *Tennyson Laureate* by Valerie Pitt (Barrie). My grateful thanks to all concerned.

Arrangement of This Edition

The poems appear in the chronological order of their composition, as far as this is known. The inquisitive reader may quite possibly find some explanatory help – about meanings, references, etc. – in the Notes. These I have segregated at the end of the book, in the belief that footnotes are distracting, and for the same reason I have put no signs in the text marking the words and passages dealt with.

Mariana

Mariana in the moated grange (*Measure for Measure*)

With blackest moss the flower-plots
    Were thickly crusted, one and all:
The rusted nails fell from the knots
    That held the pear to the gable-wall.
The broken sheds looked sad and strange:
    Unlifted was the clinking latch;
    Weeded and worn the ancient thatch
Upon the lonely moated grange.
        She only said, 'My life is dreary,
           He cometh not,' she said;
        She said, 'I am aweary, aweary,
           I would that I were dead!'

Her tears fell with the dews at even;
    Her tears fell ere the dews were dried;
She could not look on the sweet heaven,
    Either at morn or eventide.
After the flitting of the bats,
    When thickest dark did trance the sky,
    She drew her casement-curtain by,
And glanced athwart the glooming flats.
        She only said, 'The night is dreary,
           He cometh not,' she said;
        She said, 'I am aweary, aweary,
           I would that I were dead!'

Upon the middle of the night,
    Waking she heard the night-fowl crow:
The cock sung out an hour ere light:
    From the dark fen the oxen's low

Came to her: without hope of change,
    In sleep she seemed to walk forlorn,
    Till cold winds woke the gray-eyed morn
About the lonely moated grange.
        She only said, 'The day is dreary,
            He cometh not,' she said;
        She said, 'I am aweary, aweary,
            I would that I were dead!'

About a stone-cast from the wall
    A sluice with blackened waters slept,
And o'er it many, round and small,
    The clustered marish-mosses crept.
Hard by a poplar shook alway,
    All silver-green with gnarlèd bark:
    For leagues no other tree did mark
The level waste, the rounding gray.
        She only said, 'My life is dreary,
            He cometh not,' she said;
        She said, 'I am aweary, aweary,
            I would that I were dead!'

And ever when the moon was low,
    And the shrill winds were up and away,
In the white curtain, to and fro,
    She saw the gusty shadow sway.
But when the moon was very low,
    And wild winds bound within their cell,
    The shadow of the poplar fell
Upon her bed, across her brow.
        She only said, 'The night is dreary,
            He cometh not,' she said;
        She said, 'I am aweary, aweary,
            I would that I were dead!'

All day within the dreamy house,
   The doors upon their hinges creaked;
The blue fly sung in the pane; the mouse
   Behind the mouldering wainscot shrieked,
Or from the crevice peered about.
   Old faces glimmered through the doors,
   Old footsteps trod the upper floors,
Old voices called her from without.
      She only said, 'My life is dreary,
        He cometh not,' she said;
      She said, 'I am aweary, aweary,
        I would that I were dead!'

The sparrow's chirrup on the roof,
   The slow clock ticking, and the sound
Which to the wooing wind aloof
   The poplar made, did all confound
Her sense; but most she loathed the hour
   When the thick-moted sunbeam lay
   Athwart the chambers, and the day
Was sloping toward his western bower.
      Then, said she, 'I am very dreary,
        He will not come,' she said;
      She wept, 'I am aweary, aweary,
        Oh God, that I were dead!'

Song (A spirit haunts the year's last hours)

I

A spirit haunts the year's last hours
Dwelling amid these yellowing bowers:
    To himself he talks;
For at eventide, listening earnestly,
At his work you may hear him sob and sigh
    In the walks;
    Earthward he boweth the heavy stalks
Of the mouldering flowers:
  Heavily hangs the broad sunflower
    Over its grave i' the earth so chilly;
  Heavily hangs the hollyhock,
    Heavily hangs the tiger-lily.

II

The air is damp, and hushed, and close,
As a sick man's room when he taketh repose
    An hour before death;
My very heart faints and my whole soul grieves
At the moist rich smell of the rotting leaves,
    And the breath
    Of the fading edges of box beneath,
And the year's last rose.
  Heavily hangs the broad sunflower
    Over its grave i' the earth so chilly;
  Heavily hangs the hollyhock,
    Heavily hangs the tiger-lily.

The Kraken

Below the thunders of the upper deep;
Far, far beneath in the abysmal sea,
His ancient, dreamless, uninvaded sleep
The Kraken sleepeth: faintest sunlights flee
About his shadowy sides: above him swell
Huge sponges of millennial growth and height;
And far away into the sickly light,
From many a wondrous grot and secret cell
Unnumbered and enormous polypi
Winnow with giant arms the slumbering green.
There hath he lain for ages and will lie
Battening upon huge seaworms in his sleep,
Until the latter fire shall heat the deep;
Then once by man and angels to be seen,
In roaring he shall rise and on the surface die.

The Lady of Shalott

PART I

On either side the river lie
Long fields of barley and of rye,
That clothe the wold and meet the sky;
And through the field the road runs by
    To many-towered Camelot;
And up and down the people go,
Gazing where the lilies blow
Round an island there below,
    The island of Shalott.

Willows whiten, aspens quiver,
Little breezes dusk and shiver
Through the wave that runs for ever
By the island in the river
    Flowing down to Camelot.
Four gray walls, and four gray towers,
Overlook a space of flowers,
And the silent isle imbowers
    The Lady of Shalott.

By the margin, willow-veiled,
Slide the heavy barges trailed
By slow horses; and unhailed
The shallop flitteth silken-sailed
    Skimming down to Camelot:
But who hath seen her wave her hand?
Or at the casement seen her stand?
Or is she known in all the land,
    The Lady of Shalott?

Only reapers, reaping early
In among the bearded barley,
Hear a song that echoes cheerly
From the river winding clearly,
  Down to towered Camelot:
And by the moon the reaper weary,
Piling sheaves in uplands airy,
Listening, whispers ''Tis the fairy
  Lady of Shalott.'

PART II

There she weaves by night and day
A magic web with colours gay.
She has heard a whisper say,
A curse is on her if she stay
  To look down to Camelot.
She knows not what the curse may be,
And so she weaveth steadily,
And little other care hath she,
  The Lady of Shalott.

And moving through a mirror clear
That hangs before her all the year,
Shadows of the world appear.
There she sees the highway near
  Winding down to Camelot:
There the river eddy whirls,
And there the surly village-churls,
And the red cloaks of market girls,
  Pass onward from Shalott.

Sometimes a troop of damsels glad,
An abbot on an ambling pad,

Sometimes a curly shepherd-lad,
Or long-haired page in crimson clad,
   - Goes by to towered Camelot;
And sometimes through the mirror blue
The knights come riding two and two:
She hath no loyal knight and true,
    The Lady of Shalott.

But in her web she still delights
To weave the mirror's magic sights,
For often through the silent nights
A funeral, with plumes and lights
    And music, went to Camelot:
Or when the moon was overhead,
Came two young lovers lately wed;
'I am half sick of shadows,' said
    The Lady of Shalott.

PART III

A bow-shot from her bower-eaves,
He rode between the barley-sheaves,
The sun came dazzling through the leaves,
And flamed upon the brazen greaves
    Of bold Sir Lancelot.
A red-cross knight for ever kneeled
To a lady in his shield,
That sparkled on the yellow field,
    Beside remote Shalott.

The gemmy bridle glittered free,
Like to some branch of stars we see
Hung in the golden Galaxy.
The bridle bells rang merrily
    As he rode down to Camelot:

And from his blazoned baldric slung
A mighty silver bugle hung,
And as he rode his armour rung,
    Beside remote Shalott.

All in the blue unclouded weather
Thick-jewelled shone the saddle-leather,
The helmet and the helmet-feather
Burned like one burning flame together,
    As he rode down to Camelot.
As often through the purple night,
Below the starry clusters bright,
Some bearded meteor, trailing light,
    Moves over still Shalott.

His broad clear brow in sunlight glowed;
On burnished hooves his war-horse trode;
From underneath his helmet flowed
His coal-black curls as on he rode,
    As he rode down to Camelot.
From the bank and from the river
He flashed into the crystal mirror,
'Tirra lirra,' by the river
    Sang Sir Lancelot.

She left the web, she left the loom,
She made three paces through the room,
She saw the water-lily bloom,
She saw the helmet and the plume,
    She looked down to Camelot.
Out flew the web and floated wide;
The mirror cracked from side to side;
'The curse is come upon me,' cried
    The Lady of Shalott.

PART IV

In the stormy east-wind straining,
The pale yellow woods were waning,
The broad stream in his banks complaining.
Heavily the low sky raining
    Over towered Camelot;
Down she came and found a boat
Beneath a willow left afloat,
And round about the prow she wrote
    The Lady of Shalott.

And down the river's dim expanse
Like some bold seër in a trance,
Seeing all his own mischance –
With a glassy countenance
    Did she look to Camelot.
And at the closing of the day
She loosed the chain, and down she lay;
The broad stream bore her far away,
    The Lady of Shalott.

Lying, robed in snowy white
That loosely flew to left and right –
The leaves upon her falling light –
Through the noises of the night
    She floated down to Camelot:
And as the boat-head wound along
The willowy hills and fields among,
They heard her singing her last song,
    The Lady of Shalott.

Heard a carol, mournful, holy,
Chanted loudly, chanted lowly,
Till her blood was frozen slowly,
And her eyes were darkened wholly,
    Turned to towered Camelot.

For ere she reached upon the tide
The first house by the water-side,
Singing in her song she died,
    The Lady of Shalott.

Under tower and balcony,
By garden-wall and gallery,
A gleaming shape she floated by,
Dead-pale between the houses high,
    Silent into Camelot.
Out upon the wharfs they came,
Knight and burgher, lord and dame,
And round the prow they read her name,
    The Lady of Shalott.

Who is this? and what is here?
And in the lighted palace near
Died the sound of royal cheer;
And they crossed themselves for fear,
    All the knights at Camelot:
But Lancelot mused a little space;
He said, 'She has a lovely face;
God in his mercy lend her grace,
    The Lady of Shalott.'

Œnone

There lies a vale in Ida, lovelier
Than all the valleys of Ionian hills.
The swimming vapour slopes athwart the glen,
Puts forth an arm, and creeps from pine to pine,
And loiters, slowly drawn. On either hand
The lawns and meadow-ledges midway down
Hang rich in flowers, and far below them roars
The long brook falling through the cloven ravine
In cataract after cataract to the sea.
Behind the valley topmost Gargarus
Stands up and takes the morning: but in front
The gorges, opening wide apart, reveal
Troas and Ilion's columned citadel,
The crown of Troas.

              Hither came at noon
Mournful Œnone, wandering forlorn
Of Paris, once her playmate on the hills.
Her cheek had lost the rose, and round her neck
Floated her hair or seemed to float in rest.
She, leaning on a fragment twined with vine,
Sang to the stillness, till the mountain-shade
Sloped downward to her seat from the upper cliff.

'O mother Ida, many-fountained Ida,
Dear mother Ida, harken ere I die.
For now the noonday quiet holds the hill:
The grasshopper is silent in the grass:
The lizard, with his shadow on the stone,
Rests like a shadow, and the winds are dead.
The purple flower droops: the golden bee
Is lily-cradled: I alone awake.
My eyes are full of tears, my heart of love,

My heart is breaking, and my eyes are dim,
And I am all aweary of my life.

  'O mother Ida, many-fountained Ida,
Dear mother Ida, harken ere I die.
Hear me, O Earth, hear me, O Hills, O Caves
That house the cold crowned snake! O mountain brooks,
I am the daughter of a River-God,
Hear me, for I will speak, and build up all
My sorrow with my song, as yonder walls
Rose slowly to a music slowly breathed,
A cloud that gathered shape: for it may be
That, while I speak of it, a little while
My heart may wander from its deeper woe.

  'O mother Ida, many-fountained Ida,
Dear mother Ida, harken ere I die.
I waited underneath the dawning hills,
Aloft the mountain lawn was dewy-dark,
And dewy dark aloft the mountain pine:
Beautiful Paris, evil-hearted Paris,
Leading a jet-black goat white-horned, white-hooved,
Came up from reedy Simois all alone.

  'O mother Ida, harken ere I die.
Far-off the torrent called me from the cleft.
Far up the solitary morning smote
The streaks of virgin snow. With down-dropt eyes
I sat alone; white-breasted like a star
Fronting the dawn he moved: a leopard skin
Drooped from his shoulder, but his sunny hair
Clustered about his temples like a God's:
And his cheek brightened as the foam-bow brightens
When the wind blows the foam, and all my heart
Went forth to embrace him coming ere he came.

'Dear mother Ida, harken ere I die.
He smiled, and opening out his milk-white palm
Disclosed a fruit of pure Hesperian gold,
That smelt ambrosially, and while I looked
And listened, the full-flowing river of speech
Came down upon my heart.

     '"My own Œnone,
Beautiful-browed Œnone, my own soul,
Behold this fruit, whose gleaming rind ingraven
'For the most fair,' would seem to award it thine,
As lovelier than whatever Oread haunt
The knolls of Ida, loveliest in all grace
Of movement, and the charm of married brows."

'Dear mother Ida, harken ere I die.
He prest the blossom of his lips to mine
And added, "This was cast upon the board,
When all the full-faced presence of the Gods
Ranged in the halls of Peleus; whereupon
Rose feud, with question unto whom 'twere due:
But light-foot Iris brought it yester-eve,
Delivering, that to me, by common voice
Elected umpire, Herè comes today,
Pallas and Aphroditè, claiming each
This meed of fairest. Thou, within the cave
Behind yon whispering tuft of oldest pine,
Mayst well behold them unbeheld, unheard
Hear all, and see thy Paris judge of Gods."

'Dear mother Ida, harken ere I die.
It was the deep midnoon: one silvery cloud
Had lost his way between the piney sides
Of this long glen. Then to the bower they came,
Naked they came to that smooth-swarded bower,
And at their feet the crocus brake like fire,

Violet, amaracus, and asphodel,
Lotos and lilies: and a wind arose,
And overhead the wandering ivy and vine,
This way and that, in many a wild festoon
Ran riot, garlanding the gnarlèd boughs
With bunch and berry and flower through and through.

'O mother Ida, harken ere I die.
On the tree tops a crested peacock lit,
And o'er him flowed a golden cloud, and leaned
Upon him, slowly dropping fragrant dew.
Then first I heard the voice of her, to whom
Coming through Heaven, like a light that grows
Larger and clearer, with one mind the Gods
Rise up for reverence. She to Paris made
Proffer of royal power, ample rule
Unquestioned, overflowing revenue
Wherewith to embellish state, "from many a vale
And river-sundered champaign clothed with corn,
Or laboured mine undrainable of ore.
Honour," she said, "and homage, tax and toll,
From many an inland town and haven large,
Mast-thronged beneath her shadowing citadel
In glassy bays among her tallest towers."

'O mother Ida, harken ere I die.
Still she spake on and still she spake of power,
"Which in all action is the end of all;
Power fitted to the season; wisdom-bred
And throned of wisdom – from all neighbour crowns
Alliance and allegiance, till thy hand
Fail from the sceptre-staff. Such boon from me,
From me, Heaven's Queen, Paris, to thee king-born,
A shepherd all thy life but yet king-born,
Should come most welcome, seeing men, in power

Only, are likest gods, who have attained
Rest in a happy place and quiet seats
Above the thunder, with undying bliss
In knowledge of their own supremacy."

'Dear mother Ida, harken ere I die.
She ceased, and Paris held the costly fruit
Out at arm's-length, so much the thought of power
Flattered his spirit; but Pallas where she stood
Somewhat apart, her clear and bared limbs
O'erthwarted with the brazen-headed spear
Upon her pearly shoulder leaning cold,
The while, above, her full and earnest eye
Over her snow-cold breast and angry cheek
Kept watch, waiting decision, made reply.

"'Self-reverence, self-knowledge, self-control,
These three alone lead life to sovereign power.
Yet not for power (power of herself
Would come uncalled for) but to live by law,
Acting the law we live by without fear;
And, because right is right, to follow right
Were wisdom in the scorn of consequence."

'Dear mother Ida, harken ere I die.
Again she said: "I woo thee not with gifts.
Sequel of guerdon could not alter me
To fairer. Judge thou me by what I am,
So shalt thou find me fairest.
                                    Yet, indeed,
If gazing on divinity disrobed
Thy mortal eyes are frail to judge of fair,
Unbiased by self-profit, oh! rest thee sure
That I shall love thee well and cleave to thee,
So that my vigour, wedded to thy blood,

Shall strike within thy pulses, like a God's,
To push thee forward through a life of shocks,
Dangers, and deeds, until endurance grow
Sinewed with action, and the full-grown will,
Circled through all experiences, pure law,
Commeasure perfect freedom."

       'Here she ceased,
And Paris pondered, and I cried, "O Paris,
Give it to Pallas!" but he heard me not,
Or hearing would not hear me, woe is me!

 'O mother Ida, many-fountained Ida,
Dear mother Ida, harken ere I die.
Idalian Aphroditè beautiful,
Fresh as the foam, new-bathed in Paphian wells,
With rosy slender fingers backward drew
From her warm brows and bosom her deep hair
Ambrosial, golden round her lucid throat
And shoulder: from the violets her light foot
Shone rosy-white, and o'er her rounded form
Between the shadows of the vine-bunches
Floated the glowing sunlights, as she moved.

 'Dear mother Ida, harken ere I die.
She with a subtle smile in her mild eyes,
The herald of her triumph, drawing nigh
Half-whispered in his ear, "I promise thee
The fairest and most loving wife in Greece."
She spoke and laughed: I shut my sight for fear
But when I looked, Paris had raised his arm,
And I beheld great Herè's angry eyes,
As she withdrew into the golden cloud,
And I was left alone within the bower;
And from that time to this I am alone,
And I shall be alone until I die.

'Yet, mother Ida, harken ere I die.
Fairest – why fairest wife? am I not fair?
My love hath told me so a thousand times.
Methinks I must be fair, for yesterday,
When I past by, a wild and wanton pard,
Eyed like the evening star, with playful tail
Crouched fawning in the weed. Most loving is she?
Ah me, my mountain shepherd, that my arms
Were wound about thee, and my hot lips prest
Close, close to thine in that quick-falling dew
Of fruitful kisses, thick as Autumn rains
Flash in the pools of whirling Simois.

'O mother, hear me yet before I die.
They came, they cut away my tallest pines,
My tall dark pines, that plumed the craggy ledge
High over the blue gorge, and all between
The snowy peak and snow-white cataract
Fostered the callow eaglet – from beneath
Whose thick mysterious boughs in the dark morn
The panther's roar came muffled, while I sat
Low in the valley. Never, never more
Shall lone Œnone see the morning mist
Sweep through them; never see them overlaid
With narrow moon-lit slips of silver cloud,
Between the loud stream and the trembling stars.

'O mother, hear me yet before I die.
I wish that somewhere in the ruined folds,
Among the fragments tumbled from the glens,
Or the dry thickets, I could meet with her
The Abominable, that uninvited came
Into the fair Peleïan banquet-hall,
And cast the golden fruit upon the board,
And bred this change; that I might speak my mind,

And tell her to her face how much I hate
Her presence, hated both of Gods and men.

'O mother, hear me yet before I die.
Hath he not sworn his love a thousand times,
In this green valley, under this green hill,
Even on this hand, and sitting on this stone?
Sealed it with kisses? watered it with tears?
O happy tears, and how unlike to these!
O happy Heaven, how canst thou see my face?
O happy earth, how canst thou bear my weight?
O death, death, death, thou ever-floating cloud,
There are enough unhappy on this earth,
Pass by the happy souls, that love to live:
I pray thee, pass before my light of life,
And shadow all my soul, that I may die.
Thou weighest heavy on the heart within,
Weigh heavy on my eyelids: let me die.

'O mother, hear me yet before I die.
I will not die alone, for fiery thoughts
Do shape themselves within me, more and more,
Whereof I catch the issue, as I hear
Dead sounds at night come from the inmost hills,
Like footsteps upon wool. I dimly see
My far-off doubtful purpose, as a mother
Conjectures of the features of her child
Ere it is born: her child! – a shudder comes
Across me: never child be born of me,
Unblest, to vex me with his father's eyes!

'O mother, hear me yet before I die.
Hear me, O earth. I will not die alone,
Lest their shrill happy laughter come to me
Walking the cold and starless road of Death

Uncomforted, leaving my ancient love
With the Greek woman. I will rise and go
Down into Troy, and ere the stars come forth
Talk with the wild Cassandra, for she says
A fire dances before her, and a sound
Rings ever in her ears of armèd men.
What this may be I know not, but I know
That, wheresoe'er I am by night and day,
All earth and air seem only burning fire.'

The Lotos-Eaters

'Courage!' he said, and pointed toward the land,
'This mounting wave will roll us shoreward soon.'
In the afternoon they came unto a land
In which it seemèd always afternoon.
All round the coast the languid air did swoon,
Breathing like one that hath a weary dream.
Full-faced above the valley stood the moon;
And like a downward smoke, the slender stream
Along the cliff to fall and pause and fall did seem.

A land of streams! some, like a downward smoke,
Slow-dropping veils of thinnest lawn, did go;
And some through wavering lights and shadows broke,
Rolling a slumbrous sheet of foam below.
They saw the gleaming river seaward flow
From the inner land: far off, three mountain-tops,
Three silent pinnacles of agèd snow,
Stood sunset-flushed: and, dewed with showery drops,
Up-clomb the shadowy pine above the woven copse.

The charmèd sunset lingered low adown
In the red West: through mountain clefts the dale
Was seen far inland, and the yellow down
Bordered with palm, and many a winding vale
And meadow, set with slender galingale;
A land where all things always seemed the same!
And round about the keel with faces pale,
Dark faces pale against that rosy flame,
The mild-eyed melancholy Lotos-eaters came.

Branches they bore of that enchanted stem,
Laden with flower and fruit, whereof they gave
To each, but whoso did receive of them,
And taste, to him the gushing of the wave
Far far away did seem to mourn and rave
On alien shores; and if his fellow spake,
His voice was thin, as voices from the grave;
And deep-asleep he seemed, yet all awake,
And music in his ears his beating heart did make.

They sat them down upon the yellow sand,
Between the sun and moon upon the shore;
And sweet it was to dream of Fatherland,
Of child, and wife, and slave; but evermore
Most weary seemed the sea, weary the oar,
Weary the wandering fields of barren foam.
Then some one said, 'We will return no more;'
And all at once they sang, 'Our island home
Is far beyond the wave; we will no longer roam.'

CHORIC SONG

I

There is sweet music here that softer falls
Than petals from blown roses on the grass,
Or night-dews on still waters between walls
Of shadowy granite, in a gleaming pass;
Music that gentlier on the spirit lies,
Than tired eyelids upon tired eyes;
Music that brings sweet sleep down from the blissful skies.
Here are cool mosses deep,
And through the moss the ivies creep,
And in the stream the long-leaved flowers weep,
And from the craggy ledge the poppy hangs in sleep.

II

Why are we weighed upon with heaviness,
And utterly consumed with sharp distress,
While all things else have rest from weariness?
All things have rest: why should we toil alone,
We only toil, who are the first of things,
And make perpetual moan,
Still from one sorrow to another thrown:
Nor ever fold our wings,
And cease from wanderings,
Nor steep our brows in slumber's holy balm;
Nor harken what the inner spirit sings,
'There is no joy but calm!'
Why should we only toil, the roof and crown of things?

III

Lo! in the middle of the wood,
The folded leaf is wooed from out the bud
With winds upon the branch, and there
Grows green and broad, and takes no care,
Sun-steeped at noon, and in the moon
Nightly dew-fed; and turning yellow
Falls, and floats adown the air.
Lo! sweetened with the summer light,
The full-juiced apple, waxing over-mellow,
Drops in a silent autumn night.
All its allotted length of days,
The flower ripens in its place,
Ripens and fades, and falls, and hath no toil,
Fast-rooted in the fruitful soil.

IV

Hateful is the dark-blue sky,
Vaulted o'er the dark-blue sea.
Death is the end of life; ah, why
Should life all labour be?
Let us alone. Time driveth onward fast,
And in a little while our lips are dumb.
Let us alone. What is it that will last?
All things are taken from us, and become
Portions and parcels of the dreadful Past.
Let us alone. What pleasure can we have
To war with evil? Is there any peace
In ever climbing up the climbing wave?
All things have rest, and ripen toward the grave
In silence; ripen, fall and cease:
Give us long rest or death, dark death, or dreamful ease.

V

How sweet it were, hearing the downward stream,
With half-shut eyes ever to seem
Falling asleep in a half-dream!
To dream and dream, like yonder amber light,
Which will not leave the myrrh-bush on the height;
To hear each other's whispered speech;
Eating the Lotos day by day,
To watch the crisping ripples on the beach,
And tender curving lines of creamy spray;
To lend our hearts and spirits wholly
To the influence of mild-minded melancholy;
To muse and brood and live again in memory,
With those old faces of our infancy
Heaped over with a mound of grass,
Two handfuls of white dust, shut in an urn of brass!

VI

Dear is the memory of our wedded lives,
And dear the last embraces of our wives
And their warm tears: but all hath suffered change:
For surely now our household hearths are cold:
Our sons inherit us: our looks are strange:
And we should come like ghosts to trouble joy.
Or else the island princes over-bold
Have eat our substance, and the minstrel sings
Before them of the ten years' war in Troy,
And our great deeds, as half-forgotten things.
Is there confusion in the little isle?
Let what is broken so remain.
The Gods are hard to reconcile:
'Tis hard to settle order once again.
There *is* confusion worse than death,
Trouble on trouble, pain on pain,
Long labour unto agèd breath,
Sore task to hearts worn out by many wars
And eyes grown dim with gazing on the pilot-stars.

VII

But, propt on beds of amaranth and moly,
How sweet (while warm airs lull us, blowing lowly)
With half-dropt eyelid still,
Beneath a heaven dark and holy,
To watch the long bright river drawing slowly
His waters from the purple hill –
To hear the dewy echoes calling
From cave to cave through the thick-twinèd vine –
To watch the emerald-coloured water falling
Through many a woven acanthus-wreath divine!
Only to hear and see the far-off sparkling brine,
Only to hear were sweet, stretched out beneath the pine.

VIII

The Lotos blooms below the barren peak:
The Lotos blows by every winding creek:
All day the wind breathes low with mellower tone:
Through every hollow cave and alley lone
Round and round the spicy downs the yellow Lotos-dust is
    blown.
We have had enough of action, and of motion we,
Rolled to starboard, rolled to larboard, when the surge was
    seething free,
Where the wallowing monster spouted his foam-fountains in
    the sea.
Let us swear an oath, and keep it with an equal mind,
In the hollow Lotos-land to live and lie reclined
On the hills like Gods together, careless of mankind.
For they lie beside their nectar, and the bolts are hurled
Far below them in the valleys, and the clouds are lightly
    curled
Round their golden houses, girdled with the gleaming world:
Where they smile in secret, looking over wasted lands,
Blight and famine, plague and earthquake, roaring deeps and
    fiery sands,
Clanging fights, and flaming towns, and sinking ships, and
    praying hands.
But they smile, they find a music centred in a doleful song
Steaming up, a lamentation and an ancient tale of wrong,
Like a tale of little meaning though the words are strong;
Chanted from an ill-used race of men that cleave the soil,
Sow the seed, and reap the harvest with enduring toil,
Storing yearly little dues of wheat, and wine and oil;
Till they perish and they suffer – some, 'tis whispered – down
    in hell
Suffer endless anguish, others in Elysian valleys dwell,
Resting weary limbs at last on beds of asphodel.

Surely, surely, slumber is more sweet than toil, the shore
Than labour in the deep mid-ocean, wind and wave and oar;
Oh rest ye, brother mariners, we will not wander more.

Ulysses

It little profits that an idle king,
By this still hearth, among these barren crags,
Matched with an agèd wife, I mete and dole
Unequal laws unto a savage race,
That hoard, and sleep, and feed, and know not me.

I cannot rest from travel: I will drink
Life to the lees: all times I have enjoyed
Greatly, have suffered greatly, both with those
That loved me, and alone; on shore, and when
Through scudding drifts the rainy Hyades
Vext the dim sea: I am become a name;
For always roaming with a hungry heart
Much have I seen and known; cities of men
And manners, climates, councils, governments,
Myself not least, but honoured of them all;
And drunk delight of battle with my peers,
Far on the ringing plains of windy Troy.
I am a part of all that I have met;
Yet all experience is an arch wherethrough
Gleams that untravelled world, whose margin fades
For ever and for ever when I move.
How dull it is to pause, to make an end,
To rust unburnished, not to shine in use!
As though to breathe were life. Life piled on life
Were all too little, and of one to me
Little remains: but every hour is saved
From that eternal silence, something more,
A bringer of new things; and vile it were
For some three suns to store and hoard myself,
And this gray spirit yearning in desire

To follow knowledge like a sinking star,
Beyond the utmost bound of human thought.

   This is my son, mine own Telemachus,
To whom I leave the sceptre and the isle –
Well-loved of me, discerning to fulfil
This labour, by slow prudence to make mild
A rugged people, and through soft degrees
Subdue them to the useful and the good.
Most blameless is he, centred in the sphere
Of common duties, decent not to fail
In offices of tenderness, and pay
Meet adoration to my household gods,
When I am gone. He works his work, I mine.

   There lies the port; the vessel puffs her sail:
There gloom the dark broad seas. My mariners,
Souls that have toiled, and wrought, and thought with me –
That ever with a frolic welcome took
The thunder and the sunshine, and opposed
Free hearts, free foreheads – you and I are old;
Old age hath yet his honour and his toil;
Death closes all: but something ere the end,
Some work of noble note, may yet be done,
Not unbecoming men that strove with Gods.
The lights begin to twinkle from the rocks:
The long day wanes: the slow moon climbs: the deep
Moans round with many voices. Come, my friends,
'Tis not too late to seek a newer world.
Push off, and sitting well in order smite
The sounding furrows; for my purpose holds
To sail beyond the sunset, and the baths
Of all the western stars, until I die.
It may be that the gulfs will wash us down:
It may be we shall touch the Happy Isles,

And see the great Achilles, whom we knew.
Though much is taken, much abides; and though
We are not now that strength which in old days
Moved earth and heaven, that which we are, we are;
One equal temper of heroic hearts,
Made weak by time and fate, but strong in will
To strive, to seek, to find, and not to yield.

Morte d'Arthur

So all day long the noise of battle rolled
Among the mountains by the winter sea;
Until King Arthur's table, man by man,
Had fallen in Lyonnesse about their Lord,
King Arthur: then, because his wound was deep,
The bold Sir Bedivere uplifted him,
Sir Bedivere, the last of all his knights,
And bore him to a chapel nigh the field,
A broken chancel with a broken cross,
That stood on a dark strait of barren land.
On one side lay the Ocean, and on one
Lay a great water, and the moon was full.

Then spake King Arthur to Sir Bedivere:
'The sequel of today unsolders all
The goodliest fellowship of famous knights
Whereof this world holds record. Such a sleep
They sleep – the men I loved. I think that we
Shall never more, at any future time,
Delight our souls with talk of knightly deeds,
Walking about the gardens and the halls
Of Camelot, as in the days that were.
I perish by this people which I made, –
Though Merlin sware that I should come again
To rule once more – but let what will be, be,
I am so deeply smitten through the helm
That without help I cannot last till morn.
Thou therefore take my brand Excalibur,
Which was my pride: for thou rememberest how
In those old days, one summer noon, an arm
Rose up from out the bosom of the lake,
Clothed in white samite, mystic, wonderful,

Holding the sword – and how I rowed across
And took it, and have worn it, like a king:
And, wheresoever I am sung or told
In aftertime, this also shall be known:
But now delay not: take Excalibur,
And fling him far into the middle mere:
Watch what thou seëst, and lightly bring me word.'

   To him replied the bold Sir Bedivere:
'It is not meet, Sir King, to leave thee thus,
Aidless, alone, and smitten through the helm.
A little thing may harm a wounded man.
Yet I thy hest will all perform at full,
Watch what I see, and lightly bring thee word.'

   So saying, from the ruined shrine he stept
And in the moon athwart the place of tombs,
Where lay the mighty bones of ancient men,
Old knights, and over them the sea-wind sang
Shrill, chill, with flakes of foam. He, stepping down
By zig-zag paths, and juts of pointed rock,
Came on the shining levels of the lake.

   There drew he forth the brand Excalibur,
And o'er him, drawing it, the winter moon,
Brightening the skirts of a long cloud, ran forth
And sparkled keen with frost against the hilt:
For all the haft twinkled with diamond sparks,
Myriads of topaz-lights, and jacinth-work
Of subtlest jewellery. He gazed so long
That both his eyes were dazzled, as he stood,
This way and that dividing the swift mind,
In act to throw: but at the last it seemed
Better to leave Excalibur concealed
There in the many-knotted waterflags,

That whistled stiff and dry about the marge.
So strode he back slow to the wounded King.

Then spake King Arthur to Sir Bedivere:
'Hast thou performed my mission which I gave?
What is it thou hast seen? or what hast heard?'

And answer made the bold Sir Bedivere:
'I heard the ripple washing in the reeds,
And the wild water lapping on the crag.'

To whom replied King Arthur, faint and pale:
'Thou hast betrayed thy nature and thy name,
Not rendering true answer, as beseemed
Thy fëalty, nor like a noble knight:
For surer sign had followed, either hand,
Or voice, or else a motion of the mere.
This is a shameful thing for men to lie.
Yet now, I charge thee, quickly go again
As thou art lief and dear, and do the thing
I bad thee, watch, and lightly bring me word'.

Then went Sir Bedivere the second time
Across the ridge, and paced beside the mere,
Counting the dewy pebbles, fixed in thought;
But when he saw the wonder of the hilt,
How curiously and strangely chased, he smote
His palms together, and he cried aloud,

'And if indeed I cast the brand away,
Surely a precious thing, one worthy note,
Should thus be lost for ever from the earth,
Which might have pleased the eyes of many men.
What good should follow this, if this were done?
What harm, undone? deep harm to disobey,

Seeing obedience is the bond of rule.
Were it well to obey then, if a king demand
An act unprofitable, against himself?
The King is sick, and knows not what he does.
What record, or what relic of my lord
Should be to aftertime, but empty breath
And rumours of a doubt? but were this kept,
Stored in some treasure-house of mighty kings,
Some one might show it at a joust of arms,
Saying, "King Arthur's sword, Excalibur,
Wrought by the lonely maiden of the Lake.
Nine years she wrought it, sitting in the deeps
Upon the hidden bases of the hills."
So might some old man speak in the aftertime
To all the people, winning reverence.
But now much honour and much fame were lost.'

So spake he, clouded with his own conceit,
And hid Excalibur the second time,
And so strode back slow to the wounded King.

Then spoke King Arthur, breathing heavily:
'What is it thou hast seen? or what hast heard?'

And answer made the bold Sir Bedivere:
'I heard the water lapping on the crag,
And the long ripple washing in the reeds.'

To whom replied King Arthur, much in wrath:
'Ah, miserable and unkind, untrue,
Unknightly, traitor-hearted! Woe is me!
Authority forgets a dying king,
Laid widowed of the power in his eye
That bowed the will. I see thee what thou art,
For thou, the latest-left of all my knights,

In whom should meet the offices of all,
Thou wouldst betray me for the precious hilt;
Either from lust of gold, or like a girl
Valuing the giddy pleasure of the eyes.
Yet, for a man may fail in duty twice,
And the third time may prosper, get thee hence:
But, if thou spare to fling Excalibur,
I will arise and slay thee with my hands.'

Then quickly rose Sir Bedivere, and ran,
And, leaping down the ridges lightly, plunged
Among the bulrush-beds, and clutched the sword,
And strongly wheeled and threw it. The great brand
Made lightnings in the splendour of the moon,
And flashing round and round, and whirled in an arch,
Shot like a streamer of the northern morn,
Seen where the moving isles of winter shock
By night, with noises of the northern sea.
So flashed and fell the brand Excalibur:
But ere he dipt the surface, rose an arm
Clothed in white samite, mystic, wonderful,
And caught him by the hilt, and brandished him
Three times, and drew him under in the mere.
And lightly went the other to the King.

Then spoke King Arthur, drawing thicker breath:
'Now see I by thine eyes that this is done.
Speak out: what is it thou hast heard, or seen?'

And answer made the bold Sir Bedivere:
'Sir King, I closed mine eyelids, lest the gems
Should blind my purpose, for I never saw,
Nor shall see, here or elsewhere, till I die,
Not though I live three lives of mortal men,
So great a miracle as yonder hilt.

Then with both hands I flung him, wheeling him;
But when I looked again, behold an arm,
Clothed in white samite, mystic, wonderful,
That caught him by the hilt, and brandished him
Three times, and drew him under in the mere.'

And answer made King Arthur, breathing hard:
'My end draws nigh; 'tis time that I were gone.
Make broad thy shoulders to receive my weight,
And bear me to the margin; yet I fear
My wound hath taken cold, and I shall die.'
So saying, from the pavement he half rose,
Slowly, with pain, reclining on his arm,
And looking wistfully with wide blue eyes
As in a picture. Him Sir Bedivere
Remorsefully regarded through his tears,
And would have spoken, but he found not words,
Then took with care, and kneeling on one knee,
O'er both his shoulders drew the languid hands,
And rising bore him through the place of tombs.

But, as he walked, King Arthur panted hard,
Like one that feels a nightmare on his bed
When all the house is mute. So sighed the King,
Muttering and murmuring at his ear, 'Quick, quick!
I fear it is too late, and I shall die.'
But the other swiftly strode from ridge to ridge,
Clothed with his breath, and looking, as he walked,
Larger than human on the frozen hills.
He heard the deep behind him, and a cry
Before. His own thought drove him, like a goad.
Dry clashed his harness in the icy caves
And barren chasms, and all to left and right
The bare black cliff clanged round him, as he based
His feet on juts of slippery crag that rang

Sharp-smitten with the dint of armèd heels –
And on a sudden, lo! the level lake,
And the long glories of the winter moon.

  Then saw they how there hove a dusky barge,
Dark as a funeral scarf from stem to stern,
Beneath them; and descending they were ware
That all the decks were dense with stately forms
Black-stoled, black-hooded, like a dream – by these
Three Queens with crowns of gold – and from them rose
A cry that shivered to the tingling stars,
And, as it were one voice, an agony
Of lamentation, like a wind, that shrills
All night in a waste land, where no one comes,
Or hath come, since the making of the world.

  Then murmured Arthur, 'Place me in the barge,'
And to the barge they came. There those three Queens
Put forth their hands, and took the King, and wept.
But she, that rose the tallest of them all
And fairest, laid his head upon her lap,
And loosed the shattered casque, and chafed his hands,
And called him by his name, complaining loud,
And dropping bitter tears against his brow
Striped with dark blood: for all his face was white
And colourless, and like the withered moon
Smote by the fresh beam of the springing east;
And all his greaves and cuisses dashed with drops
Of onset; and the light and lustrous curls –
That made his forehead like a rising sun
High from the daïs-throne – were parched with dust;
Or, clotted into points and hanging loose,
Mixed with the knightly growth that fringed his lips.
So like a shattered column lay the King;
Not like that Arthur who, with lance in rest,

From spur to plume a star of tournament,
Shot through the lists at Camelot, and charged
Before the eyes of ladies and of kings.

   Then loudly cried the bold Sir Bedivere,
'Ah! my Lord Arthur, whither shall I go?
Where shall I hide my forehead and my eyes?
For now I see the true old times are dead,
When every morning brought a noble chance,
And every chance brought out a noble knight.
Such times have been not since the light that led
The holy Elders with the gift of myrrh.
But now the whole ROUND TABLE is dissolved
Which was an image of the mighty world;
And I, the last, go forth companionless,
And the days darken round me, and the years,
Among new men, strange faces, other minds.'

   And slowly answered Arthur from the barge:
'The old order changeth, yielding place to new,
And God fulfils Himself in many ways,
Lest one good custom should corrupt the world.
Comfort thyself: what comfort is in me?
I have lived my life, and that which I have done
May He within Himself make pure! but thou,
If thou shouldst never see my face again,
Pray for my soul. More things are wrought by prayer
Than this world dreams of. Wherefore, let thy voice
Rise like a fountain for me night and day.
For what are men better than sheep or goats
That nourish a blind life within the brain,
If, knowing God, they lift not hands of prayer
Both for themselves and those who call them friend?
For so the whole round earth is every way
Bound by gold chains about the feet of God.

But now farewell. I am going a long way
With these thou seëst – if indeed I go –
(For all my mind is clouded with a doubt)
To the island-valley of Avilion;
Where falls not hail, or rain, or any snow,
Nor ever wind blows loudly; but it lies
Deep-meadowed, happy, fair with orchard-lawns
And bowery hollows crowned with summer sea,
Where I will heal me of my grievous wound.'

  So said he, and the barge with oar and sail
Moved from the brink, like some full-breasted swan
That, fluting a wild carol ere her death,
Ruffles her pure cold plume, and takes the flood
With swarthy webs. Long stood Sir Bedivere
Revolving many memories, till the hull
Looked one black dot against the verge of dawn,
And on the mere the wailing died away.

'Break, break, break'

Break, break, break,
  On thy cold gray stones, O Sea!
And I would that my tongue could utter
  The thoughts that arise in me.

O well for the fisherman's boy,
  That he shouts with his sister at play!
O well for the sailor lad,
  That he sings in his boat on the bay!

And the stately ships go on
  To their haven under the hill;
But O for the touch of a vanished hand,
  And the sound of a voice that is still!

Break, break, break,
  At the foot of thy crags, O Sea!
But the tender grace of a day that is dead
  Will never come back to me.

Will Waterproof's Lyrical Monologue

Made at The Cock

O plump head-waiter at The Cock,
   To which I most resort,
How goes the time? 'Tis five o'clock.
   Go fetch a pint of port:
But let it not be such as that
   You set before chance-comers,
But such whose father-grape grew fat
   On Lusitanian summers.

No vain libation to the Muse,
   But may she still be kind,
And whisper lovely words, and use
   Her influence on the mind,
To make me write my random rhymes,
   Ere they be half-forgotten;
Nor add and alter, many times,
   Till all be ripe and rotten.

I pledge her, and she comes and dips
   Her laurel in the wine,
And lays it thrice upon my lips,
   These favoured lips of mine;
Until the charm have power to make
   New lifeblood warm the bosom,
And barren commonplaces break
   In full and kindly blossom.

I pledge her silent at the board;
   Her gradual fingers steal
And touch upon the master-chord
   Of all I felt and feel.

Old wishes, ghosts of broken plans,
   And phantom hopes assemble;
And that child's heart within the man's
   Begins to move and tremble.

Through many an hour of summer suns,
   By many pleasant ways,
Against its fountain upward runs
   The current of my days:
I kiss the lips I once have kissed;
   The gas-light wavers dimmer;
And softly, through a vinous mist,
   My college friendships glimmer.

I grow in worth, and wit, and sense,
   Unboding critic-pen,
Or that eternal want of pence,
   Which vexes public men,
Who hold their hands to all, and cry
   For that which all deny them –
Who sweep the crossings, wet or dry,
   And all the world go by them.

Ah yet, though all the world forsake,
   Though fortune clip my wings,
I will not cramp my heart, nor take
   Half-views of men and things.
Let Whig and Tory stir their blood;
   There must be stormy weather;
But for some true result of good
   All parties work together.

Let there be thistles, there are grapes;
   If old things, there are new;
Ten thousand broken lights and shapes,
   Yet glimpses of the true.

Let raffs be rife in prose and rhyme,
   We lack not rhymes and reasons,
As on this whirligig of Time
   We circle with the seasons.

This earth is rich in man and maid;
   With fair horizons bound:
This whole wide earth of light and shade
   Comes out a perfect round.
High over roaring Temple-bar,
   And set in Heaven's third story,
I look at all things as they are,
   But through a kind of glory.

———————

Head-waiter, honoured by the guest
   Half-mused, or reeling ripe,
The pint, you brought me, was the best
   That ever came from pipe.
But though the port surpasses praise,
   My nerves have dealt with stiffer.
Is there some magic in the place?
   Or do my peptics differ?

For since I came to live and learn,
   No pint of white or red
Had ever half the power to turn
   This wheel within my head,
Which bears a seasoned brain about,
   Unsubject to confusion,
Though soaked and saturate, out and out,
   Through every convolution.

For I am of a numerous house,
  With many kinsmen gay,
Where long and largely we carouse
  As who shall say me nay:
Each month, a birth-day coming on,
  We drink defying trouble,
Or sometimes two would meet in one,
  And then we drank it double;

Whether the vintage, yet unkept,
  Had relish fiery-new,
Or elbow-deep in sawdust, slept,
  As old as Waterloo;
Or stowed, when classic Canning died,
  In musty bins and chambers,
Had cast upon its crusty side
  The gloom of ten Decembers.

The Muse, the jolly Muse, it is!
  She answered to my call,
She changes with that mood or this,
  Is all-in-all to all:
She lit the spark within my throat,
  To make my blood run quicker,
Used all her fiery will, and smote
  Her life into the liquor.

And hence this halo lives about
  The waiter's hands, that reach
To each his perfect pint of stout,
  His proper chop to each.
He looks not like the common breed
  That with the napkin dally;
I think he came like Ganymede,
  From some delightful valley.

The Cock was of a larger egg
   Than modern poultry drop,
Stept forward on a firmer leg,
   And crammed a plumper crop;
Upon an ampler dunghill trod,
   Crowed lustier late and early,
Sipt wine from silver, praising God,
   And raked in golden barley.

A private life was all his joy,
   Till in a court he saw
A something-pottle-bodied boy
   That knuckled at the taw:
He stooped and clutched him, fair and good,
   Flew over roof and casement:
His brothers of the weather stood
   Stock-still for sheer amazement.

But he, by farmstead, thorpe and spire,
   And followed with acclaims,
A sign to many a staring shire
   Came crowing over Thames.
Right down by smoky Paul's they bore,
   Till, where the street grows straiter,
One fixed for ever at the door,
   And one became head-waiter.

———————

But whither would my fancy go?
   How out of place she makes
The violet of a legend blow
   Among the chops and steaks!
'Tis but a steward of the can,
   One shade more plump than common;
As just and mere a serving-man
   As any born of woman.

I ranged too high: what draws me down
   Into the common day?
Is it the weight of that half-crown,
   Which I shall have to pay?
For, something duller than at first,
   Nor wholly comfortable,
I sit, my empty glass reversed,
   And thrumming on the table:

Half fearful that, with self at strife,
   I take myself to task;
Lest of the fulness of my life
   I leave an empty flask:
For I had hope, by something rare,
   To prove myself a poet:
But, while I plan and plan, my hair
   Is gray before I know it.

So fares it since the years began,
   Till they be gathered up;
The truth, that flies the flowing can,
   Will haunt the vacant cup:
And others' follies teach us not,
   Nor much their wisdom teaches;
And most, of sterling worth, is what
   Our own experience preaches.

Ah, let the rusty theme alone!
   We know not what we know.
But for my pleasant hour, 'tis gone;
   'Tis gone, and let it go.
'Tis gone: a thousand such have slipt
   Away from my embraces,
And fallen into the dusty crypt
   Of darkened forms and faces.

Go, therefore, thou! thy betters went
   Long since, and came no more;
With peals of genial clamour sent
   From many a tavern-door,
With twisted quirks and happy hits,
   From misty men of letters;
The tavern-hours of mighty wits –
   Thine elders and thy betters.

Hours, when the Poet's words and looks
   Had yet their native glow:
Nor yet the fear of little books
   Had made him talk for show;
But, all his vast heart sherris-warmed,
   He flashed his random speeches,
Ere days, that deal in ana, swarmed
   His literary leeches.

So mix for ever with the past,
   Like all good things on earth!
For should I prize thee, couldst thou last,
   At half thy real worth?
I hold it good, good things should pass:
   With time I will not quarrel:
It is but yonder empty glass
   That makes me maudlin-moral.

———

Head-waiter of the chop-house here,
   To which I most resort,
I too must part: I hold thee dear
   For this good pint of port.
For this, thou shalt from all things suck
   Marrow of mirth and laughter;
And wheresoe'er thou move, good luck
   Shall fling her old shoe after.

But thou wilt never move from hence,
   The sphere thy fate allots:
Thy latter days increased with pence
   Go down among the pots:
Thou battenest by the greasy gleam
   In haunts of hungry sinners,
Old boxes, larded with the steam
   Of thirty thousand dinners.

We fret, we fume, would shift our skins,
   Would quarrel with our lot;
Thy care is, under polished tins,
   To serve the hot-and-hot;
To come and go, and come again,
   Returning like the pewit,
And watched by silent gentlemen,
   That trifle with the cruet.

Live long, ere from thy topmost head
   The thick-set hazel dies;
Long, ere the hateful crow shall tread
   The corners of thine eyes:
Live long, nor feel in head or chest
   Our changeful equinoxes,
Till mellow Death, like some late guest,
   Shall call thee from the boxes.

But when he calls, and thou shalt cease
   To pace the gritted floor,
And, laying down an unctuous lease
   Of life, shalt earn no more;
No carved cross-bones, the types of Death,
   Shall show thee past to Heaven:
But carved cross-pipes, and, underneath,
   A pint-pot neatly graven.

Locksley Hall

Comrades, leave me here a little, while as yet 'tis early morn:
Leave me here, and when you want me, sound upon the
  bugle-horn.

'Tis the place, and all around it, as of old, the curlews call,
Dreary gleams about the moorland flying over Locksley Hall;

Locksley Hall, that in the distance overlooks the sandy tracts,
And the hollow ocean-ridges roaring into cataracts.

Many a night from yonder ivied casement, ere I went to rest,
Did I look on great Orion sloping slowly to the West.

Many a night I saw the Pleiads, rising through the mellow
  shade,
Glitter like a swarm of fire-flies tangled in a silver braid.

Here about the beach I wandered, nourishing a youth sublime
With the fairy tales of science, and the long result of Time;

When the centuries behind me like a fruitful land reposed;
When I clung to all the present for the promise that it closed:

When I dipt into the future far as human eye could see;
Saw the Vision of the world, and all the wonder that would
  be. –

In the Spring a fuller crimson comes upon the robin's breast;
In the Spring the wanton lapwing gets himself another crest;

In the Spring a livelier iris changes on the burnished dove;
In the Spring a young man's fancy lightly turns to thoughts
  of love.

Then her cheek was pale and thinner than should be for one
    so young,
And her eyes on all my motions with a mute observance hung.

And I said, 'My cousin Amy, speak, and speak the truth to
    me,
Trust me, cousin, all the current of my being sets to thee.'

On her pallid cheek and forehead came a colour and a light,
As I have seen the rosy red flushing in the northern night.

And she turned – her bosom shaken with a sudden storm of
    sighs –
All the spirit deeply dawning in the dark of hazel eyes –

Saying, 'I have hid my feelings, fearing they should do me
    wrong;'
Saying, 'Dost thou love me, cousin?' weeping, 'I have loved
    thee long.'

Love took up the glass of Time, and turned it in his glowing
    hands;
Every moment, lightly shaken, ran itself in golden sands.

Love took up the harp of Life, and smote on all the chords
    with might;
Smote the chord of Self, that, trembling, passed in music out
    of sight.

Many a morning on the moorland did we hear the copses ring,
And her whisper thronged my pulses with the fulness of the
    Spring.

Many an evening by the waters did we watch the stately ships,
And our spirits rushed together at the touching of the lips.

O my cousin, shallow-hearted! O my Amy, mine no more!
O the dreary, dreary moorland! O the barren, barren shore!

Falser than all fancy fathoms, falser than all songs have sung,
Puppet to a father's threat, and servile to a shrewish tongue!

Is it well to wish thee happy? – having known me – to decline
On a range of lower feelings and a narrower heart than mine!

Yet it shall be: thou shalt lower to his level day by day,
What is fine within thee growing coarse to sympathise with
    clay.

As the husband is, the wife is: thou art mated with a clown,
And the grossness of his nature will have weight to drag thee
    down.

He will hold thee, when his passion shall have spent its novel
    force,
Something better than his dog, a little dearer than his horse.

What is this? his eyes are heavy: think not they are glazed
    with wine.
Go to him: it is thy duty: kiss him: take his hand in thine.

It may be my lord is weary, that his brain is overwrought:
Soothe him with thy finer fancies, touch him with thy lighter
    thought.

He will answer to the purpose, easy things to understand –
Better thou wert dead before me, though I slew thee with my
    hand!

Better thou and I were lying, hidden from the heart's dis-
    grace,
Rolled in one another's arms, and silent in a last embrace.

Cursèd be the social wants that sin against the strength of
   youth!
Cursèd be the social lies that warp us from the living truth!

Cursèd be the sickly forms that err from honest Nature's rule!
Cursèd be the gold that gilds the straitened forehead of the
   fool!

Well – 'tis well that I should bluster! – Hadst thou less un-
   worthy proved –
Would to God – for I had loved thee more than ever wife was
   loved..

Am I mad, that I should cherish that which bears but bitter
   fruit?
I will pluck it from my bosom, though my heart be at the root.

Never, though my mortal summers to such length of years
   should come
As the many-wintered crow that leads the clanging rookery
   home.

Where is comfort? in division of the records of the mind?
Can I part her from herself, and love her, as I knew her, kind?

I remember one that perished: sweetly did she speak and
   move:
Such a one do I remember, whom to look at was to love.

Can I think of her as dead, and love her for the love she bore?
No – she never loved me truly: love is love for evermore.

Comfort? comfort scorned of devils! this is truth the poet
   sings,
That a sorrow's crown of sorrow is remembering happier
   things.

Drug thy memories, lest thou learn it, lest thy heart be put
  to proof,
In the dead unhappy night, and when the rain is on the roof.

Like a dog, he hunts in dreams, and thou art staring at the
  wall,
Where the dying night-lamp flickers, and the shadows rise
  and fall.

Then a hand shall pass before thee, pointing to his drunken
  sleep,
To thy widowed marriage-pillows, to the tears that thou wilt
  weep.

Thou shalt hear the 'Never, never,' whispered by the
  phantom years,
And a song from out the distance in the ringing of thine ears;

And an eye shall vex thee, looking ancient kindness on thy
  pain.
Turn thee, turn thee on thy pillow: get thee to thy rest again.

Nay, but Nature brings thee solace; for a tender voice will
  cry.
'Tis a purer life than thine; a lip to drain thy trouble dry.

Baby lips will laugh me down: my latest rival brings thee rest.
Baby fingers, waxen touches, press me from the mother's
  breast.

O, the child too clothes the father with a dearness not his due.
Half is thine and half is his: it will be worthy of the two.

O, I see thee old and formal, fitted to thy petty part,
With a little hoard of maxims preaching down a daughter's
  heart.

'They were dangerous guides the feelings – she herself was
    not exempt –
Truly, she herself had suffered' – Perish in thy self-contempt!

Overlive it – lower yet – be happy! wherefore should I care?
I myself must mix with action, lest I wither by despair.

What is that which I should turn to, lighting upon days like
    these?
Every door is barred with gold, and opens but to golden keys.

Every gate is thronged with suitors, all the markets overflow.
I have but an angry fancy: what is that which I should do?

I had been content to perish, falling on the foeman's ground,
When the ranks are rolled in vapour, and the winds are laid
    with sound.

But the jingling of the guinea helps the hurt that Honour feels,
And the nations do but murmur, snarling at each other's heels.

Can I but relive in sadness? I will turn that earlier page.
Hide me from my deep emotion, O thou wondrous Mother-
    Age!

Make me feel the wild pulsation that I felt before the strife,
When I heard my days before me, and the tumult of my life;

Yearning for the large excitement that the coming years
    would yield,
Eager-hearted as a boy when first he leaves his father's field,

And at night along the dusky highway near and nearer drawn,
Sees in heaven the light of London flaring like a dreary dawn;

And his spirit leaps within him to be gone before him then,
Underneath the light he looks at, in among the throngs of
    men:

Men, my brothers, men the workers, ever reaping something
    new:
That which they have done but earnest of the things that they
    shall do:

For I dipt into the future, far as human eye could see,
Saw the Vision of the world, and all the wonder that would be;

Saw the heavens fill with commerce, argosies of magic sails,
Pilots of the purple twilight, dropping down with costly bales;

Heard the heavens fill with shouting, and there rained a
    ghastly dew
From the nations' airy navies grappling in the central blue;

Far along the world-wide whisper of the south-wind rushing
    warm,
With the standards of the peoples plunging through the
    thunder-storm;

Till the war-drum throbbed no longer, and the battle-flags
    were furled
In the Parliament of man, the Federation of the world.

There the common sense of most shall hold a fretful realm in
    awe,
And the kindly earth shall slumber, lapt in universal law.

So I triumphed ere my passion sweeping through me left me
    dry,
Left me with the palsied heart, and left me with the jaundiced
    eye;

Eye, to which all order festers, all things here are out of joint:
Science moves, but slowly slowly, creeping on from point to
  point:

Slowly comes a hungry people, as a lion creeping nigher,
Glares at one that nods and winks behind a slowly-dying fire.

Yet I doubt not through the ages one increasing purpose runs,
And the thoughts of men are widened with the process of the
  suns.

What is that to him that reaps not harvest of his youthful joys,
Though the deep heart of existence beat for ever like a boy's?

Knowledge comes, but wisdom lingers, and I linger on the
  shore,
And the individual withers, and the world is more and more.

Knowledge comes, but wisdom lingers, and he bears a laden
  breast,
Full of sad experience, moving toward the stillness of his rest.

Hark, my merry comrades call me, sounding on the bugle-
  horn,
They to whom my foolish passion were a target for their
  scorn:

Shall it not be scorn to me to harp on such a mouldered
  string?
I am shamed through all my nature to have loved so slight a
  thing.

Weakness to be wroth with weakness! woman's pleasure,
  woman's pain –
Nature made them blinder motions bounded in a shallower
  brain:

Woman is the lesser man, and all thy passions, matched with
  mine,
Are as moonlight unto sunlight, and as water unto wine –

Here at least, where nature sickens, nothing. Ah, for some
  retreat
Deep in yonder shining Orient, where my life began to beat;

Where in wild Mahratta-battle fell my father evil-starred; –
I was left a trampled orphan, and a selfish uncle's ward.

Or to burst all links of habit – there to wander far away,
On from island unto island at the gateways of the day.

Larger constellations burning, mellow moons and happy
  skies,
Breadths of tropic shade and palms in cluster, knots of
  Paradise.

Never comes the trader, never floats an European flag,
Slides the bird o'er lustrous woodland, swings the trailer from
  the crag;

Droops the heavy-blossomed bower, hangs the heavy-fruited
  tree –
Summer isles of Eden lying in dark-purple spheres of sea.

There methinks would be enjoyment more than in this march
  of mind,
In the steamship, in the railway, in the thoughts that shake
  mankind.

There the passions cramped no longer shall have scope and
  breathing space;
I will take some savage woman, she shall rear my dusky race.

Iron jointed, supple-sinewed, they shall dive, and they shall
run,
Catch the wild goat by the hair, and hurl their lances in the
sun;

Whistle back the parrot's call, and leap the rainbows of the
brooks,
Not with blinded eyesight poring over miserable books –

Fool, again the dream, the fancy! but I *know* my words are
wild,
But I count the gray barbarian lower than the Christian child.

I, to herd with narrow foreheads, vacant of our glorious gains,
Like a beast with lower pleasures, like a beast with lower
pains!

Mated with a squalid savage – what to me were sun or clime?
I the heir of all the ages, in the foremost files of time –

I that rather held it better men should perish one by one,
Than that earth should stand at gaze like Joshua's moon in
Ajalon!

Not in vain the distance beacons. Forward, forward let us
range,
Let the great world spin for ever down the ringing grooves of
change.

Through the shadow of the globe we sweep into the younger
day:
Better fifty years of Europe than a cycle of Cathay.

Mother-Age (for mine I knew not) help me as when life
    begun:
Rift the hills, and roll the waters, flash the lightnings, weigh
    the Sun.

O, I see the crescent promise of my spirit hath not set.
Ancient founts of inspiration well through all my fancy yet.

Howsoever these things be, a long farewell to Locksley Hall!
Now for me the woods may wither, now for me the roof-tree
    fall.

Comes a vapour from the margin, blackening over heath and
    holt,
Cramming all the blast before it, in its breast a thunderbolt.

Let it fall on Locksley Hall, with rain or hail, or fire or snow;
For the mighty wind arises, roaring seaward, and I go.

'Come not, when I am dead'

Come not, when I am dead,
   To drop thy foolish tears upon my grave,
To trample round my fallen head,
   And vex the unhappy dust thou wouldst not save.
There let the wind sweep and the plover cry;
      But thou, go by.

Child, if it were thine error or thy crime
   I care no longer, being all unblest:
Wed whom thou wilt, but I am sick of Time,
   And I desire to rest.
Pass on, weak heart, and leave me where I lie:
      Go by, go by.

Songs from *The Princess*

I

'Tears, idle tears, I know not what they mean,
Tears from the depth of some divine despair
Rise in the heart, and gather to the eyes,
In looking on the happy Autumn-fields,
And thinking of the days that are no more.
    'Fresh as the first beam glittering on a sail,

That brings our friends up from the underworld,
Sad as the last which reddens over one
That sinks with all we love below the verge;
So sad, so fresh, the days that are no more.

    'Ah, sad and strange as in dark summer dawns
The earliest pipe of half-awakened birds
To dying ears, when unto dying eyes
The casement slowly grows a glimmering square;
So sad, so strange, the days that are no more.

    'Dear as remembered kisses after death,
And sweet as those by hopeless fancy feigned
On lips that are for others; deep as love,
Deep as first love, and wild with all regret;
O Death in Life, the days that are no more.'

II

'O Swallow, Swallow, flying, flying South,
Fly to her, and fall upon her gilded eaves,
And tell her, tell her, what I tell to thee.

    'O tell her, Swallow, thou that knowest each,
That bright and fierce and fickle is the South,
And dark and true and tender is the North.

'O Swallow, Swallow, if I could follow, and light
Upon her lattice, I would pipe and trill,
And cheep and twitter twenty million loves.

'O were I thou that she might take me in,
And lay me on her bosom, and her heart
Would rock the snowy cradle till I died.

'Why lingereth she to clothe her heart with love,
Delaying as the tender ash delays
To clothe herself, when all the woods are green?

'O tell her, Swallow, that thy brood is flown:
Say to her, I do but wanton in the South,
But in the North long since my nest is made.

'O tell her, brief is life but love is long,
And brief the sun of summer in the North,
And brief the moon of beauty in the South.

'O Swallow, flying from the golden woods,
Fly to her, and pipe and woo her, and make her mine,
And tell her, tell her, that I follow thee.'

III

'Now sleeps the crimson petal, now the white;
Nor waves the cypress in the palace walk;
Nor winks the gold fin in the porphyry font:
The fire-fly wakens: waken thou with me.

Now droops the milkwhite peacock like a ghost,
And like a ghost she glimmers on to me.

Now lies the Earth all Danaë to the stars,
And all thy heart lies open unto me.

Now slides the silent meteor on, and leaves
A shining furrow, as thy thoughts in me.

Now folds the lily all her sweetness up,
And slips into the bosom of the lake:
So fold thyself, my dearest, thou, and slip
Into my bosom and be lost in me.'

IV

'Come down, O maid, from yonder mountain height:
What pleasure lives in height (the shepherd sang)
In height and cold, the splendour of the hills?
But cease to move so near the Heavens, and cease
To glide a sunbeam by the blasted Pine,
To sit a star upon the sparkling spire;
And come, for Love is of the valley, come,
For Love is of the valley, come thou down
And find him; by the happy threshold, he,
Or hand in hand with Plenty in the maize,
Or red with spirted purple of the vats,
Or foxlike in the vine; nor cares to walk
With Death and Morning on the silver horns,
Nor wilt thou snare him in the white ravine,
Nor find him dropt upon the firths of ice,
That huddling slant in furrow-cloven falls
To roll the torrent out of dusky doors:
But follow; let the torrent dance thee down
To find him in the valley; let the wild
Lean-headed Eagles yelp alone, and leave
The monstrous ledges there to slope, and spill
Their thousand wreaths of dangling water-smoke,
That like a broken purpose waste in air:
So waste not thou; but come; for all the vales
Await thee; azure pillars of the hearth
Arise to thee; the children call, and I

Thy shepherd pipe, and sweet is every sound,
Sweeter thy voice, but every sound is sweet;
Myriads of rivulets hurrying through the lawn,
The moan of doves in immemorial elms,
And murmuring of innumerable bees.'

V

Sweet and low, sweet and low,
   Wind of the western sea,
Low, low, breathe and blow,
   Wind of the western sea!
Over the rolling waters go,
Come from the dying moon, and blow,
   Blow him again to me;
While my little one, while my pretty one, sleeps.

Sleep and rest, sleep and rest,
   Father will come to thee soon;
Rest, rest, on mother's breast,
   Father will come to thee soon;
Father will come to his babe in the nest,
Silver sails all out of the west
   Under the silver moon:
Sleep, my little one, sleep, my pretty one, sleep.

VI

   The splendour falls on castle walls
      And snowy summits old in story:
   The long light shakes across the lakes,
      And the wild cataract leaps in glory.
Blow, bugle, blow, set the wild echoes flying,
Blow, bugle; answer, echoes, dying, dying, dying.

O hark, O hear! how thin and clear,
    And thinner, clearer, farther going!
O sweet and far from cliff and scar
    The horns of Elfland faintly blowing!
Blow, let us hear the purple glens replying:
Blow, bugle; answer, echoes, dying, dying, dying.

O love, they die in yon rich sky,
    They faint on hill or field or river:
Our echoes roll from soul to soul,
    And grow for ever and for ever.
Blow, bugle, blow, set the wild echoes flying,
And answer, echoes, answer, dying, dying, dying.

VII

Ask me no more: the moon may draw the sea;
    The cloud may stoop from heaven and take the shape
    With fold to fold, of mountain or of cape;
But O too fond, when have I answered thee?
                    Ask me no more.

Ask me no more: what answer should I give?
    I love not hollow cheek or faded eye:
    Yet, O my friend, I will not have thee die!
Ask me no more, lest I should bid thee live;
                    Ask me no more.

Ask me no more: thy fate and mine are sealed:
    I strove against the stream and all in vain:
    Let the great river take me to the main:
No more, dear love, for at a touch I yield;
                    Ask me no more.

In Memoriam A. H. H.

Strong Son of God, immortal Love,
    Whom we, that have not seen thy face,
    By faith, and faith alone, embrace,
Believing where we cannot prove;

Thine are these orbs of light and shade;
    Thou madest Life in man and brute;
    Thou madest Death; and lo, thy foot
Is on the skull which thou hast made.

Thou wilt not leave us in the dust:
    Thou madest man, he knows not why,
    He thinks he was not made to die;
And thou hast made him: thou art just.

Thou seemest human and divine,
    The highest, holiest manhood, thou:
    Our wills are ours, we know not how;
Our wills are ours, to make them thine.

Our little systems have their day;
    They have their day and cease to be:
    They are but broken lights of thee,
And thou, O Lord, art more than they.

We have but faith: we cannot know;
    For knowledge is of things we see;
    And yet we trust it comes from thee,
A beam in darkness: let it grow.

Let knowledge grow from more to more,
  But more of reverence in us dwell;
  That mind and soul, according well,
May make one music as before,

But vaster. We are fools and slight;
  We mock thee when we do not fear:
  But help thy foolish ones to bear;
Help thy vain worlds to bear thy light.

Forgive what seemed my sin in me;
  What seemed my worth since I began;
  For merit lives from man to man,
And not from man, O Lord, to thee.

Forgive my grief for one removed,
  Thy creature, whom I found so fair.
  I trust he lives in thee, and there
I find him worthier to be loved.

Forgive these wild and wandering cries,
  Confusions of a wasted youth;
  Forgive them where they fail in truth,
And in thy wisdom make me wise.

                              1849

I

I held it truth, with him who sings
  To one clear harp in divers tones,
  That men may rise on stepping-stones
Of their dead selves to higher things.

But who shall so forecast the years
   And find in loss a gain to match?
   Or reach a hand through time to catch
The far-off interest of tears?

Let Love clasp Grief lest both be drowned,
   Let darkness keep her raven gloss:
   Ah, sweeter to be drunk with loss,
To dance with death, to beat the ground,

Than that the victor Hours should scorn
   The long result of love, and boast,
   'Behold the man that loved and lost,
But all he was is overworn.'

II

Old Yew, which graspest at the stones
   That name the under-lying dead,
   Thy fibres net the dreamless head,
Thy roots are wrapt about the bones.

The seasons bring the flower again,
   And bring the firstling to the flock;
   And in the dusk of thee, the clock
Beats out the little lives of men.

O not for thee the glow, the bloom,
   Who changest not in any gale,
   Nor branding summer suns avail
To touch thy thousand years of gloom:

And gazing on thee, sullen tree,
   Sick for thy stubborn hardihood,
   I seem to fail from out my blood
And grow incorporate into thee.

III

O Sorrow, cruel fellowship,
  O Priestess in the vaults of Death,
  O sweet and bitter in a breath,
What whispers from thy lying lip?

'The stars,' she whispers, 'blindly run;
  A web is woven across the sky;
  From out waste places comes a cry,
And murmurs from the dying sun:

'And all the phantom, Nature, stands –
  With all the music in her tone,
  A hollow echo of my own, –
A hollow form with empty hands.'

And shall I take a thing so blind,
  Embrace her as my natural good;
  Or crush her, like a vice of blood,
Upon the threshold of the mind?

IV

To Sleep I give my powers away;
  My will is bondsman to the dark;
  I sit within a helmless bark,
And with my heart I muse and say:

O heart, how fares it with thee now,
  That thou should'st fail from thy desire,
  Who scarcely darest to inquire,
'What is it makes me beat so low?'

Something it is which thou hast lost,
   Some pleasure from thine early years.
   Break, thou deep vase of chilling tears,
That grief hath shaken into frost!

Such clouds of nameless trouble cross
   All night below the darkened eyes;
   With morning wakes the will, and cries,
'Thou shalt not be the fool of loss.'

V

I sometimes hold it half a sin
   To put in words the grief I feel;
   For words, like Nature, half reveal
And half conceal the Soul within.

But, for the unquiet heart and brain,
   A use in measured language lies;
   The sad mechanic exercise,
Like dull narcotics, numbing pain.

In words, like weeds, I'll wrap me o'er,
   Like coarsest clothes against the cold:
   But that large grief which these enfold
Is given in outline and no more.

VI

One writes, that 'Other friends remain,'
   That 'Loss is common to the race' –
   And common is the commonplace,
And vacant chaff well meant for grain.

That loss is common would not make
   My own less bitter, rather more:
   Too common! Never morning wore
To evening, but some heart did break.

O father, wheresoe'er thou be,
   Who pledgest now thy gallant son;
   A shot, ere half thy draught be done,
Hath stilled the life that beat from thee.

O mother, praying God will save
   Thy sailor, – while thy head is bowed,
   His heavy-shotted hammock-shroud
Drops in his vast and wandering grave.

Ye know no more than I who wrought
   At that last hour to please him well;
   Who mused on all I had to tell,
And something written, something thought;

Expecting still his advent home;
   And ever met him on his way
   With wishes, thinking, 'here today,'
Or 'here tomorrow will he come.'

O somewhere, meek, unconscious dove,
   That sittest ranging golden hair;
   And glad to find thyself so fair,
Poor child, that waitest for thy love!

For now her father's chimney glows
   In expectation of a guest;
   And thinking 'this will please him best,'
She takes a riband or a rose;

For he will see them on tonight;
   And with the thought her colour burns;
   And, having left the glass, she turns
Once more to set a ringlet right;

And, even when she turned, the curse
   Had fallen, and her future Lord
   Was drowned in passing through the ford,
Or killed in falling from his horse.

O what to her shall be the end?
   And what to me remains of good?
   To her, perpetual maidenhood,
And unto me no second friend.

VII

Dark house, by which once more I stand
   Here in the long unlovely street,
   Doors, where my heart was used to beat
So quickly, waiting for a hand,

A hand that can be clasped no more –
   Behold me, for I cannot sleep,
   And like a guilty thing I creep
At earliest morning to the door.

He is not here; but far away
   The noise of life begins again,
   And ghastly through the drizzling rain
On the bald street breaks the blank day.

VIII

A happy lover who has come
  To look on her that loves him well,
  Who 'lights and rings the gateway bell,
And learns her gone and far from home;

He saddens, all the magic light
  Dies off at once from bower and hall,
  And all the place is dark, and all
The chambers emptied of delight:

So find I every pleasant spot
  In which we two were wont to meet,
  The field, the chamber and the street,
For all is dark where thou art not.

Yet as that other, wandering there
  In those deserted walks, may find
  A flower beat with rain and wind,
Which once she fostered up with care;

So seems it in my deep regret,
  O my forsaken heart, with thee
  And this poor flower of poesy
Which little cared for fades not yet.

But since it pleased a vanished eye,
  I go to plant it on his tomb,
  That if it can it there may bloom,
Or dying, there at least may die.

IX

Fair ship, that from the Italian shore
   Sailest the placid ocean-plains
   With my lost Arthur's loved remains,
Spread thy full wings, and waft him o'er.

So draw him home to those that mourn
   In vain; a favourable speed
   Ruffle thy mirrored mast, and lead
Through prosperous floods his holy urn.

All night no ruder air perplex
   Thy sliding keel, till Phosphor, bright
   As our pure love, through early light
Shall glimmer on the dewy decks.

Sphere all your lights around, above;
   Sleep, gentle heavens, before the prow;
   Sleep, gentle winds, as he sleeps now,
My friend, the brother of my love;

My Arthur, whom I shall not see
   Till all my widowed race be run;
   Dear as the mother to the son,
More than my brothers are to me.

X

I hear the noise about thy keel;
   I hear the bell struck in the night:
   I see the cabin-window bright;
I see the sailor at the wheel.

Thou bring'st the sailor to his wife,
    And travelled men from foreign lands;
    And letters unto trembling hands;
And, thy dark freight, a vanished life.

So bring him: we have idle dreams:
    This look of quiet flatters thus
    Our home-bred fancies: O to us,
The fools of habit, sweeter seems

To rest beneath the clover sod,
    That takes the sunshine and the rains,
    Or where the kneeling hamlet drains
The chalice of the grapes of God;

Than if with thee the roaring wells
    Should gulf him fathom-deep in brine;
    And hands so often clasped in mine,
Should toss with tangle and with shells.

XI

Calm is the morn without a sound,
    Calm as to suit a calmer grief,
    And only through the faded leaf
The chestnut pattering to the ground:

Calm and deep peace on this high wold,
    And on these dews that drench the furze,
    And all the silvery gossamers
That twinkle into green and gold:

Calm and still light on yon great plain
    That sweeps with all its autumn bowers,
    And crowded farms and lessening towers,
To mingle with the bounding main:

Calm and deep peace in this wide air,
  These leaves that redden to the fall;
  And in my heart, if calm at all,
If any calm, a calm despair:

Calm on the seas, and silver sleep,
  And waves that sway themselves in rest,
  And dead calm in that noble breast
Which heaves but with the heaving deep.

XII

Lo, as a dove when up she springs
  To bear through Heaven a tale of woe,
  Some dolorous message knit below
The wild pulsation of her wings;

Like her I go; I cannot stay;
  I leave this mortal ark behind,
  A weight of nerves without a mind,
And leave the cliffs, and haste away

O'er ocean-mirrors rounded large,
  And reach the glow of southern skies,
  And see the sails at distance rise,
And linger weeping on the marge,

And saying; 'Comes he thus, my friend?
  Is this the end of all my care?'
  And circle moaning in the air:
'Is this the end? Is this the end?'

And forward dart again, and play
  About the prow, and back return
  To where the body sits, and learn
That I have been an hour away.

XIII

Tears of the widower, when he sees
   A late-lost form that sleep reveals,
   And moves his doubtful arms, and feels
Her place is empty, fall like these;

Which weep a loss for ever new,
   A void where heart on heart reposed;
   And, where warm hands have prest and closed,
Silence, till I be silent too.

Which weep the comrade of my choice,
   An awful thought, a life removed,
   The human-hearted man I loved,
A Spirit, not a breathing voice.

Come Time, and teach me, many years,
   I do not suffer in a dream;
   For now so strange do these things seem,
Mine eyes have leisure for their tears;

My fancies time to rise on wing,
   And glance about the approaching sails,
   As though they brought but merchants' bales,
And not the burthen that they bring.

XIV

If one should bring me this report,
   That thou hadst touched the land today,
   And I went down unto the quay,
And found thee lying in the port;

And standing, muffled round with woe,
  Should see thy passengers in rank
   Come stepping lightly down the plank,
And beckoning unto those they know;

And if along with these should come
  The man I held as half-divine;
   Should strike a sudden hand in mine,
And ask a thousand things of home;

And I should tell him all my pain,
  And how my life had drooped of late,
   And he should sorrow o'er my state
And marvel what possessed my brain;

And I perceived no touch of change,
  No hint of death in all his frame,
   But found him all in all the same,
I should not feel it to be strange.

XV

Tonight the winds begin to rise
  And roar from yonder dropping day:
   The last red leaf is whirled away,
The rooks are blown about the skies;

The forest cracked, the waters curled,
  The cattle huddled on the lea;
   And wildly dashed on tower and tree
The sunbeam strikes along the world:

And but for fancies, which aver
  That all thy motions gently pass
   Athwart a plane of molten glass,
I scarce could brook the strain and stir

That makes the barren branches loud;
   And but for fear it is not so,
   The wild unrest that lives in woe
Would dote and pore on yonder cloud

That rises upward always higher,
   And onward drags a labouring breast,
   And topples round the dreary west,
A looming bastion fringed with fire.

XVI

What words are these have fallen from me?
   Can calm despair and wild unrest
   Be tenants of a single breast,
Or sorrow such a changeling be?

Or doth she only seem to take
   The touch of change in calm or storm;
   But knows no more of transient form
In her deep self, than some dead lake

That holds the shadow of a lark
   Hung in the shadow of a heaven?
   Or has the shock, so harshly given,
Confused me like the unhappy bark

That strikes by night a craggy shelf,
   And staggers blindly ere she sink?
   And stunned me from my power to think
And all my knowledge of myself;

And made me that delirious man
   Whose fancy fuses old and new,
   And flashes into false and true,
And mingles all without a plan?

XVII

Thou comest, much wept for: such a breeze
  Compelled thy canvas, and my prayer
  Was as the whisper of an air
To breathe thee over lonely seas.

For I in spirit saw thee move
  Through circles of the bounding sky,
  Week after week: the days go by:
Come quick, thou bringest all I love.

Henceforth, wherever thou mayst roam,
  My blessing, like a line of light,
  Is on the waters day and night,
And like a beacon guards thee home.

So may whatever tempest mars
  Mid-ocean, spare thee, sacred bark;
  And balmy drops in summer dark
Slide from the bosom of the stars.

So kind an office hath been done,
  Such precious relics brought by thee;
  The dust of him I shall not see
Till all my widowed race be run.

XVIII

'Tis well; 'tis something; we may stand
  Where he in English earth is laid,
  And from his ashes may be made
The violet of his native land.

'Tis little; but it looks in truth
  As if the quiet bones were blest
  Among familiar names to rest
And in the places of his youth.

Come then, pure hands, and bear the head
  That sleeps or wears the mask of sleep,
  And come, whatever loves to weep,
And hear the ritual of the dead.

Ah yet, even yet, if this might be,
  I, falling on his faithful heart,
  Would breathing through his lips impart
The life that almost dies in me;

That dies not, but endures with pain,
  And slowly forms the firmer mind,
  Treasuring the look it cannot find,
The words that are not heard again.

XIX

The Danube to the Severn gave
  The darkened heart that beat no more;
  They laid him by the pleasant shore,
And in the hearing of the wave.

There twice a day the Severn fills;
  The salt sea-water passes by,
  And hushes half the babbling Wye,
And makes a silence in the hills.

The Wye is hushed nor moved along,
  And hushed my deepest grief of all,
  When filled with tears that cannot fall,
I brim with sorrow drowning song.

The tide flows down, the wave again
   Is vocal in its wooded walls;
   My deeper anguish also falls,
And I can speak a little then.

XX

The lesser griefs that may be said,
   That breathe a thousand tender vows,
   Are but as servants in a house
Where lies the master newly dead;

Who speak their feeling as it is,
   And weep the fulness from the mind:
   'It will be hard,' they say, 'to find
Another service such as this.'

My lighter moods are like to these,
   That out of words a comfort win;
   But there are other griefs within,
And tears that at their fountain freeze;

For by the hearth the children sit
   Cold in that atmosphere of Death,
   And scarce endure to draw the breath,
Or like to noiseless phantoms flit:

But open converse is there none,
   So much the vital spirits sink
   To see the vacant chair, and think,
'How good! how kind! and he is gone.'

XXI

I sing to him that rests below,
   And, since the grasses round me wave,
   I take the grasses of the grave,
And make them pipes whereon to blow.

The traveller hears me now and then,
   And sometimes harshly will he speak:
   'This fellow would make weakness weak,
And melt the waxen hearts of men.'

Another answers, 'Let him be,
   He loves to make parade of pain,
   That with his piping he may gain
The praise that comes to constancy.'

A third is wroth: 'Is this an hour
   For private sorrow's barren song,
   When more and more the people throng
The chairs and thrones of civil power?

'A time to sicken and to swoon,
   When Science reaches forth her arms
   To feel from world to world, and charms
Her secret from the latest moon?'

Behold, ye speak an idle thing:
   Ye never knew the sacred dust:
   I do but sing because I must,
And pipe but as the linnets sing:

And one is glad; her note is gay,
   For now her little ones have ranged;
   And one is sad: her note is changed,
Because her brood is stolen away.

XXII

The path by which we twain did go,
   Which led by tracts that pleased us well,
   Through four sweet years arose and fell,
From flower to flower, from snow to snow:

And we with singing cheered the way,
   And, crowned with all the season lent,
   From April on to April went,
And glad at heart from May to May:

But where the path we walked began
   To slant the fifth autumnal slope,
   As we descended following Hope,
There sat the Shadow feared of man;

Who broke our fair companionship,
   And spread his mantle dark and cold,
   And wrapt thee formless in the fold,
And dulled the murmur on thy lip,

And bore thee where I could not see
   Nor follow, though I walk in haste,
   And think, that somewhere in the waste
The Shadow sits and waits for me.

XXIII

Now, sometimes in my sorrow shut,
   Or breaking into song by fits,
   Alone, alone, to where he sits,
The Shadow cloaked from head to foot,

Who keeps the keys of all the creeds,
    I wander, often falling lame,
    And looking back to whence I came,
Or on to where the pathway leads;

And crying, How changed from where it ran
    Through lands where not a leaf was dumb;
    But all the lavish hills would hum
The murmur of a happy Pan:

When each by turns was guide to each,
    And Fancy light from Fancy caught,
    And Thought leapt out to wed with Thought
Ere Thought could wed itself with Speech;

And all we met was fair and good,
    And all was good that Time could bring,
    And all the secret of the Spring
Moved in the chambers of the blood;

And many an old philosophy
    On Argive heights divinely sang,
    And round us all the thicket rang
To many a flute of Arcady.

XXIV

And was the day of my delight
    As pure and perfect as I say?
    The very source and fount of Day
Is dashed with wandering isles of night.

If all was good and fair we met,
    This earth had been the Paradise
    It never looked to human eyes
Since our first Sun arose and set.

And is it that the haze of grief
   Makes former gladness loom so great?
   The lowness of the present state,
That sets the past in this relief?

Or that the past will always win
   A glory from its being far;
   And orb into the perfect star
We saw not, when we moved therein?

XXV

I know that this was Life, – the track
   Whereon with equal feet we fared;
   And then, as now, the day prepared
The daily burden for the back.

But this it was that made me move
   As light as carrier-birds in air;
   I loved the weight I had to bear,
Because it needed help of Love:

Nor could I weary, heart or limb,
   When mighty Love would cleave in twain
   The lading of a single pain,
And part it, giving half to him.

XXVI

Still onward winds the dreary way;
   I with it; for I long to prove
   No lapse of moons can canker Love,
Whatever fickle tongues may say.

And if that eye which watches guilt
   And goodness, and hath power to see
   Within the green the mouldered tree,
And towers fallen as soon as built –

Oh, if indeed that eye foresee
   Or see (in Him is no before)
   In more of life true life no more
And Love the indifference to be,

Then might I find, ere yet the morn
   Breaks hither over Indian seas,
   That Shadow waiting with the keys,
To shroud me from my proper scorn.

XXVII

I envy not in any moods
   The captive void of noble rage,
   The linnet born within the cage,
That never knew the summer woods:

I envy not the beast that takes
   His license in the field of time,
   Unfettered by the sense of crime,
To whom a conscience never wakes;

Nor, what may count itself as blest,
   The heart that never plighted troth
   But stagnates in the weeds of sloth;
Nor any want-begotten rest.

I hold it true, whate'er befall;
   I feel it, when I sorrow most;
   'Tis better to have loved and lost
Than never to have loved at all.

XXVIII

The time draws near the birth of Christ:
   The moon is hid; the night is still;
   The Christmas bells from hill to hill
Answer each other in the mist.

Four voices of four hamlets round,
   From far and near, on mead and moor,
   Swell out and fail, as if a door
Were shut between me and the sound:

Each voice four changes on the wind,
   That now dilate, and now decrease,
   Peace and goodwill, goodwill and peace,
Peace and goodwill, to all mankind.

This year I slept and woke with pain,
   I almost wished no more to wake,
   And that my hold on life would break
Before I heard those bells again:

But they my troubled spirit rule,
   For they controlled me when a boy;
   They bring me sorrow touched with joy,
The merry merry bells of Yule.

XXIX

With such compelling cause to grieve
   As daily vexes household peace,
   And chains regret to his decease,
How dare we keep our Christmas-eve;

Which brings no more a welcome guest
   To enrich the threshold of the night
   With showered largess of delight
In dance and song and game and jest?

Yet go, and while the holly boughs
   Entwine the cold baptismal font,
   Make one wreath more for Use and Wont,
That guard the portals of the house;

Old sisters of a day gone by,
   Gray nurses, loving nothing new;
   Why should they miss their yearly due
Before their time? They too will die.

XXX

With trembling fingers did we weave
   The holly round the Christmas hearth;
   A rainy cloud possessed the earth,
And sadly fell our Christmas-eve.

At our old pastimes in the hall
   We gambolled, making vain pretence
   Of gladness, with an awful sense
Of one mute Shadow watching all.

We paused: the winds were in the beech:
   We heard them sweep the winter land;
   And in a circle hand-in-hand
Sat silent, looking each at each.

Then echo-like our voices rang;
   We sung, though every eye was dim,
   A merry song we sang with him
Last year: impetuously we sang:

We ceased: a gèntler feeling crept
   Upon us: surely rest is meet:
   'They rest,' we said, 'their sleep is sweet,'
And silence followed, and we wept.

Our voices took a higher range;
   Once more we sang: 'They do not die
   Nor lose their mortal sympathy,
Nor change to us, although they change;

'Rapt from the fickle and the frail
   With gathered power, yet the same,
   Pierces the keen seraphic flame
From orb to orb, from veil to veil.'

Rise, happy morn, rise, holy morn,
   Draw forth the cheerful day from night:
   O Father, touch the east, and light
The light that shone when Hope was born.

XXXI

When Lazarus left his charnel-cave,
   And home to Mary's house returned,
   Was this demanded – if he yearned
To hear her weeping by his grave?

'Where wert thou, brother, those four days?'
   There lives no record of reply,
   Which telling what it is to die
Had surely added praise to praise.

From every house the neighbours met,
   The streets were filled with joyful sound,
   A solemn gladness even crowned
The purple brows of Olivet.

Behold a man raised up by Christ!
   The rest remaineth unrevealed;
   He told it not; or something sealed
The lips of that Evangelist.

XXXII

Her eyes are homes of silent prayer,
   Nor other thought her mind admits
   But, he was dead, and there he sits,
And he that brought him back is there.

Then one deep love doth supersede
   All other, when her ardent gaze
   Roves from the living brother's face,
And rests upon the Life indeed.

All subtle thought, all curious fears,
   Borne down by gladness so complete,
   She bows, she bathes the Saviour's feet
With costly spikenard and with tears.

Thrice blest whose lives are faithful prayers,
   Whose loves in higher love endure;
   What souls possess themselves so pure,
Or is there blessedness like theirs?

XXXIII

O thou that after toil and storm
   Mayst seem to have reached a purer air,
   Whose faith has centre everywhere,
Nor cares to fix itself to form,

Leave thou thy sister when she prays,
   Her early Heaven, her happy views;
   Nor thou with shadowed hint confuse
A life that leads melodious days.

Her faith through form is pure as thine,
   Her hands are quicker unto good:
   Oh, sacred be the flesh and blood
To which she links a truth divine!

See thou, that countest reason ripe
   In holding by the law within,
   Thou fail not in a world of sin,
And even for want of such a type.

XXXIV

My own dim life should teach me this,
   That life shall live for evermore,
   Else earth is darkness at the core,
And dust and ashes all that is;

This round of green, this orb of flame,
   Fantastic beauty; such as lurks
   In some wild Poet, when he works
Without a conscience or an aim.

What then were God to such as I?
   'Twere hardly worth my while to choose
   Of things all mortal, or to use
A little patience ere I die;

'Twere best at once to sink to peace,
   Like birds the charming serpent draws,
   To drop head-foremost in the jaws
Of vacant darkness and to cease.

XXXV

Yet if some voice that man could trust
   Should murmur from the narrow house,
   'The cheeks drop in; the body bows;
Man dies: nor is there hope in dust:'

Might I not say? 'Yet even here,
   But for one hour, O Love, I strive
   To keep so sweet a thing alive:'
But I should turn mine ears and hear

The moanings of the homeless sea,
   The sound of streams that swift or slow
   Draw down Æonian hills, and sow
The dust of continents to be;

And Love would answer with a sigh,
   'The sound of that forgetful shore
   Will change my sweetness more and more,
Half-dead to know that I shall die.'

O me, what profits it to put
   An idle case? If Death were seen
   At first as Death, Love had not been,
Or been in narrowest working shut,

Mere fellowship of sluggish moods,
   Or in his coarsest Satyr-shape
   Had bruised the herb and crushed the grape,
And basked and battened in the woods.

XXXVI

Though truths in manhood darkly join,
    Deep-seated in our mystic frame,
    We yield all blessing to the name
Of Him that made them current coin;

For Wisdom dealt with mortal powers,
    Where truth in closest words shall fail,
    When truth embodied in a tale
Shall enter in at lowly doors.

And so the Word had breath, and wrought
    With human hands the creed of creeds
    In loveliness of perfect deeds,
More strong than all poetic thought;

Which he may read that binds the sheaf,
    Or builds the house, or digs the grave,
    And those wild eyes that watch the wave
In roarings round the coral reef.

XXXVII

Urania speaks with darkened brow:
    'Thou pratest here where thou art least;
    This faith has many a purer priest,
And many an abler voice than thou.

'Go down beside thy native rill,
    On thy Parnassus set thy feet,
    And hear thy laurel whisper sweet
About the ledges of the hill.'

And my Melpomene replies,
   A touch of shame upon her cheek:
   'I am not worthy even to speak
Of thy prevailing mysteries;

'For I am but an earthly Muse,
   And owning but a little art
   To lull with song an aching heart,
And render human love his dues;

'But brooding on the dear one dead,
   And all he said of things divine,
   (And dear to me as sacred wine
To dying lips is all he said),

'I murmured, as I came along,
   Of comfort clasped in truth revealed;
   And loitered in the master's field,
And darkened sanctities with song.'

XXXVIII

With weary steps I loiter on,
   Though always under altered skies
   The purple from the distance dies,
My prospect and horizon gone.

No joy the blowing season gives,
   The herald melodies of spring,
   But in the songs I love to sing
A doubtful gleam of solace lives.

If any care for what is here
   Survive in spirits rendered free,
   Then are these songs I sing of thee
Not all ungrateful to thine ear.

XXXIX

Old warder of these buried bones,
   And answering now my random stroke
   With fruitful cloud and living smoke,
Dark yew, that graspest at the stones

And dippest toward the dreamless head,
   To thee too comes the golden hour
   When flower is feeling after flower;
But Sorrow – fixt upon the dead,

And darkening the dark graves of men, –
   What whispered from her lying lips?
   Thy gloom is kindled at the tips,
And passes into gloom again.

XL

Could we forget the widowed hour
   And look on Spirits breathed away,
   As on a maiden in the day
When first she wears her orange-flower!

When crowned with blessing she doth rise
   To take her latest leave of home,
   And hopes and light regrets that come
Make April of her tender eyes;

And doubtful joys the father move,
   And tears are on the mother's face,
   As parting with a long embrace
She enters other realms of love;

Her office there to rear, to teach,
   Becoming as is meet and fit
   A link among the days, to knit
The generations each with each;

And, doubtless, unto thee is given
   A life that bears immortal fruit
   In those great offices that suit
The full-grown energies of heaven.

Ay me, the difference I discern!
   How often shall her old fireside
   Be cheered with tidings of the bride,
How often she herself return,

And tell them all they would have told,
   And bring her babe, and make her boast,
   Till even those that missed her most
Shall count new things as dear as old:

But thou and I have shaken hands,
   Till growing winters lay me low;
   My paths are in the fields I know,
And thine in undiscovered lands.

XLI

Thy spirit ere our fatal loss
   Did ever rise from high to higher;
   As mounts the heavenward altar-fire,
As flies the lighter through the gross.

But thou art turned to something strange,
   And I have lost the links that bound
   Thy changes; here upon the ground,
No more partaker of thy change.

Deep folly! yet that this could be –
 That I could wing my will with might
 To leap the grades of life and light,
And flash at once, my friend, to thee.

For though my nature rarely yields
 To that vague fear implied in death;
 Nor shudders at the gulfs beneath,
The howlings from forgotten fields;

Yet oft when sundown skirts the moor
 An inner trouble I behold,
 A spectral doubt which makes me cold,
That I shall be thy mate no more,

Though following with an upward mind
 The wonders that have come to thee,
 Through all the secular to-be,
But evermore a life behind.

XLII

I vex my heart with fancies dim:
 He still outstript me in the race;
 It was but unity of place
That made me dream I ranked with him.

And so may Place retain us still,
 And he the much-beloved again,
 A lord of large experience, train
To riper growth the mind and will:

And what delights can equal those
 That stir the spirit's inner deeps,
 When one that loves but knows not, reaps
A truth from one that loves and knows?

XLIII

If Sleep and Death be truly one,
  And every spirit's folded bloom
  Through all its intervital gloom
In some long trance should slumber on;

Unconscious of the sliding hour,
  Bare of the body, might it last,
  And silent traces of the past
Be all the colour of the flower:

So then were nothing lost to man;
  So that still garden of the souls
  In many a figured leaf enrolls
The total world since life began;

And love will last as pure and whole
  As when he loved me here in Time,
  And at the spiritual prime
Rewaken with the dawning soul.

XLIV

How fares it with the happy dead?
  For here the man is more and more;
  But he forgets the days before
God shut the doorways of his head.

The days have vanished, tone and tint,
  And yet perhaps the hoarding sense
  Gives out at times (he knows not whence)
A little flash, a mystic hint;

And in the long harmonious years
   (If Death so taste Lethean springs),
   May some dim touch of earthly things
Surprise thee ranging with thy peers.

If such a dreamy touch should fall,
   O turn thee round, resolve the doubt;
   My guardian angel will speak out
In that high place, and tell thee all.

XLV

The baby new to earth and sky,
   What time his tender palm is prest
   Against the circle of the breast,
Has never thought that 'this is I:'

But as he grows he gathers much,
   And learns the use of 'I', and 'me',
   And finds 'I am not what I see,
And other than the things I touch.'

So rounds he to a separate mind
   From whence clear memory may begin,
   As through the frame that binds him in
His isolation grows defined.

This use may lie in blood and breath,
   Which else were fruitless of their due,
   Had man to learn himself anew
Beyond the second birth of Death.

XLVI

We ranging down this lower track,
    The path we came by, thorn and flower,
    Is shadowed by the growing hour,
Lest life should fail in looking back.

So be it: there no shade can last
    In that deep dawn behind the tomb,
    But clear from marge to marge shall bloom
The eternal landscape of the past;

A lifelong tract of time revealed;
    The fruitful hours of still increase;
    Days ordered in a wealthy peace,
And those five years its richest field.

O Love, thy province were not large,
    A bounded field, nor stretching far;
    Look also, Love, a brooding star,
A rosy warmth from marge to marge.

XLVII

That each, who seems a separate whole,
    Should move his rounds, and fusing all
    The skirts of self again, should fall
Remerging in the general Soul,

Is faith as vague as all unsweet:
    Eternal form shall still divide
    The eternal soul from all beside;
And I shall know him when we meet:

And we shall sit at endless feast,
    Enjoying each the other's good:
    What vaster dream can hit the mood
Of Love on earth? He seeks at least

Upon the last and sharpest height,
    Before the spirits fade away,
    Some landing-place, to clasp and say,
'Farewell! We lose ourselves in light.'

XLVIII

If these brief lays, of Sorrow born,
    Were taken to be such as closed
    Grave doubts and answers here proposed,
Then these were such as men might scorn:

Her care is not to part and prove;
    She takes, when harsher moods remit,
    What slender shade of doubt may flit,
And makes it vassal unto love:

And hence, indeed, she sports with words,
    But better serves a wholesome law,
    And holds it sin and shame to draw
The deepest measure from the chords:

Nor dare she trust a larger lay,
    But rather loosens from the lip
    Short swallow-flights of song, that dip
Their wings in tears, and skim away.

XLIX

From art, from nature, from the schools,
    Let random influences glance,
    Like light in many a shivered lance
That breaks about the dappled pools:

The lightest wave of thought shall lisp,
    The fancy's tenderest eddy wreathe,
    The slightest air of song shall breathe
To make the sullen surface crisp.

And look thy look, and go thy way,
    But blame not thou the winds that make
    The seeming-wanton ripple break,
The tender-pencilled shadow play.

Beneath all fancied hopes and fears
    Ay me, the sorrow deepens down,
    Whose muffled motions blindly drown
The bases of my life in tears.

L

Be near me when my light is low,
    When the blood creeps, and the nerves prick
    And tingle; and the heart is sick,
And all the wheels of Being slow.

Be near me when the sensuous frame
    Is racked with pangs that conquer trust;
    And Time, a maniac scattering dust,
And Life, a Fury slinging flame.

Be near me when my faith is dry,
   And men the flies of latter spring,
   That lay their eggs, and sting and sing
And weave their petty cells and die.

Be near me when I fade away,
   To point the term of human strife,
   And on the low dark verge of life
The twilight of eternal day.

LI

Do we indeed desire the dead
   Should still be near us at our side?
   Is there no baseness we would hide?
No inner vileness that we dread?

Shall he for whose applause I strove,
   I had such reverence for his blame,
   See with clear eye some hidden shame
And I be lessened in his love?

I wrong the grave with fears untrue:
   Shall love be blamed for want of faith?
   There must be wisdom with great Death:
The dead shall look me through and through.

Be near us when we climb or fall:
   Ye watch, like God, the rolling hours
   With larger other eyes than ours,
To make allowance for us all.

LII

I cannot love thee as I ought,
  For love reflects the thing beloved;
  My words are only words, and moved
Upon the topmost froth of thought.

'Yet blame not thou thy plaintive song,'
  The Spirit of true love replied;
  'Thou canst not move me from thy side,
Nor human frailty do me wrong.

'What keeps a spirit wholly true
  To that ideal which he bears?
  What record? not the sinless years
That breathed beneath the Syrian blue:

'So fret not, like an idle girl,
  That life is dashed with flecks of sin.
  Abide: thy wealth is gathered in,
When Time hath sundered shell from pearl.'

LIII

How many a father have I seen,
  A sober man, among his boys,
  Whose youth was full of foolish noise,
Who wears his manhood hale and green:

And dare we to this fancy give,
  That had the wild oat not been sown,
  The soil, left barren, scarce had grown
The grain by which a man may live?

Or, if we held the doctrine sound
  For life outliving heats of youth,
  Yet who would preach it as a truth
To those that eddy round and round?

Hold thou the good: define it well:
  For fear divine Philosophy
  Should push beyond her mark, and be
Procuress to the Lords of Hell.

LIV

Oh yet we trust that somehow good
  Will be the final goal of ill,
  To pangs of nature, sins of will,
Defects of doubt, and taints of blood;

That nothing walks with aimless feet;
  That not one life shall be destroyed,
  Or cast as rubbish to the void,
When God hath made the pile complete;

That not a worm is cloven in vain;
  That not a moth with vain desire
  Is shrivelled in a fruitless fire,
Or but subserves another's gain.

Behold, we know not anything;
  I can but trust that good shall fall
  At last – far off – at last, to all,
And every winter change to spring.

So runs my dream: but what am I?
  An infant crying in the night:
  An infant crying for the light:
And with no language but a cry.

LV

The wish, that of the living whole
   No life may fail beyond the grave,
   Derives it not from what we have
The likest God within the soul?

Are God and Nature then at strife,
   That Nature lends such evil dreams?
   So careful of the type she seems,
So careless of the single life;

That I, considering everywhere
   Her secret meaning in her deeds,
   And finding that of fifty seeds
She often brings but one to bear,

I falter where I firmly trod,
   And falling with my weight of cares
   Upon the great world's altar-stairs
That slope through darkness up to God,

I stretch lame hands of faith, and grope,
   And gather dust and chaff, and call
   To what I feel is Lord of all,
And faintly trust the larger hope.

LVI

'So careful of the type?' but no.
   From scarpèd cliff and quarried stone
   She cries, 'A thousand types are gone:
I care for nothing, all shall go.

'Thou makest thine appeal to me:
　I bring to life, I bring to death:
　The spirit does but mean the breath:
I know no more.' And he, shall he,

Man, her last work, who seemed so fair,
　Such splendid purpose in his eyes,
　Who rolled the psalm to wintry skies,
Who built him fanes of fruitless prayer,

Who trusted God was love indeed
　And love Creation's final law –
　Though Nature, red in tooth and claw
With ravine, shrieked against his creed –

Who loved, who suffered countless ills,
　Who battled for the True, the Just,
　Be blown about the desert dust,
Or sealed within the iron hills?

No more? A monster then, a dream,
　A discord. Dragons of the prime,
　That tare each other in their slime,
Were mellow music matched with him.

O life as futile, then, as frail!
　O for thy voice to soothe and bless!
　What hope of answer or redress?
Behind the veil, behind the veil.

LVII

Peace; come away: the song of woe
　Is after all an earthly song:
　Peace; come away: we do him wrong
To sing so wildly: let us go.

Come; let us go: your cheeks are pale;
   But half my life I leave behind:
   Methinks my friend is richly shrined;
But I shall pass; my work will fail.

Yet in these ears, till hearing dies,
   One set slow bell will seem to toll
   The passing of the sweetest soul
That ever looked with human eyes.

I hear it now, and o'er and o'er,
   Eternal greetings to the dead;
   And 'Ave, Ave, Ave,' said,
'Adieu, adieu' for evermore.

LVIII

In those sad words I took farewell:
   Like echoes in sepulchral halls,
   As drop by drop the water falls
In vaults and catacombs, they fell;

And, falling, idly broke the peace
   Of hearts that beat from day to day,
   Half-conscious of their dying clay,
And those cold crypts where they shall cease.

The high Muse answered: 'Wherefore grieve
   Thy brethren with a fruitless tear?
   Abide a little longer here,
And thou shalt take a nobler leave.'

LIX

O Sorrow, wilt thou live with me
   No casual mistress, but a wife,
   My bosom-friend and half of life;
As I confess it needs must be;

O Sorrow, wilt thou rule my blood,
   Be sometimes lovely like a bride,
   And put thy harsher moods aside,
If thou wilt have me wise and good.

My centred passion cannot move,
   Nor will it lessen from today;
   But I'll have leave at times to play
As with the creature of my love;

And set thee forth, for thou art mine,
   With so much hope for years to come,
   That, howsoe'er I know thee, some
Could hardly tell what name were thine.

LX

He past; a soul of nobler tone:
   My spirit loved and loves him yet,
   Like some poor girl whose heart is set
On one whose rank exceeds her own.

He mixing with his proper sphere,
   She finds the baseness of her lot,
   Half jealous of she knows not what,
And envying all that meet him there.

The little village looks forlorn;
   She sighs amid her narrow days,
   Moving about the household ways,
In that dark house where she was born.

The foolish neighbours come and go,
   And tease her till the day draws by:
   At night she weeps, 'How vain am I!
How should he love a thing so low?'

LXI

If, in thy second state sublime,
   Thy ransomed reason change replies
   With all the circle of the wise,
The perfect flower of human time;

And if thou cast thine eyes below,
   How dimly charactered and slight,
   How dwarfed a growth of cold and night,
How blanched with darkness must I grow!

Yet turn thee to the doubtful shore,
   Where thy first form was made a man;
   I loved thee, Spirit, and love, nor can
The soul of Shakspeare love thee more.

LXII

Though if an eye that's downward cast
   Could make thee somewhat blench or fail,
   Then be my love an idle tale,
And fading legend of the past;

And thou, as one that once declined,
    When he was little more than boy,
    On some unworthy heart with joy,
But lives to wed an equal mind;

And breathes a novel world, the while
    His other passion wholly dies,
    Or in the light of deeper eyes
Is matter for a flying smile.

LXIII

Yet pity for a horse o'er-driven,
    And love in which my hound has part,
    Can hang no weight upon my heart
In its assumptions up to heaven;

And I am so much more than these,
    As thou, perchance, art more than I,
    And yet I spare them sympathy,
And I would set their pains at ease.

So mayst thou watch me where I weep,
    As, unto vaster motions bound,
    The circuits of thine orbit round
A higher height, a deeper deep.

LXIV

Dost thou look back on what hath been,
    As some divinely gifted man,
    Whose life in low estate began
And on a simple village green;

Who breaks his birth's invidious bar,
   And grasps the skirts of happy chance,
   And breasts the blows of circumstance,
And grapples with his evil star;

Who makes by force his merit known
   And lives to clutch the golden keys,
   To mould a mighty state's decrees,
And shape the whisper of the throne;

And moving up from high to higher,
   Becomes on Fortune's crowning slope
   The pillar of a people's hope,
The centre of a world's desire;

Yet feels, as in a pensive dream,
   When all his active powers are still,
   A distant dearness in the hill,
A secret sweetness in the stream,

The limit of his narrower fate,
   While yet beside its vocal springs
   He played at counsellors and kings,
With one that was his earliest mate;

Who ploughs with pain his native lea
   And reaps the labour of his hands,
   Or in the furrow musing stands;
'Does my old friend remember me?'

LXV

Sweet soul, do with me as thou wilt;
   I lull a fancy trouble-tost
   With 'Love's too precious to be lost,
A little grain shall not be spilt.'

And in that solace can I sing,
    Till out of painful phases wrought
    There flutters up a happy thought,
Self-balanced on a lightsome wing:

Since we deserved the name of friends,
    And thine effect so lives in me,
    A part of mine may live in thee
And move thee on to noble ends.

LXVI

You thought my heart too far diseased;
    You wonder when my fancies play
    To find me gay among the gay,
Like one with any trifle pleased.

The shade by which my life was crost,
    Which makes a desert in the mind,
    Has made me kindly with my kind,
And like to him whose sight is lost;

Whose feet are guided through the land,
    Whose jest among his friends is free,
    Who takes the children on his knee,
And winds their curls about his hand:

He plays with threads, he beats his chair
    For pastime, dreaming of the sky;
    His inner day can never die,
His night of loss is always there.

LXVII

When on my bed the moonlight falls,
 I know that in thy place of rest
 By that broad water of the west,
There comes a glory on the walls;

Thy marble bright in dark appears,
 As slowly steals a silver flame
 Along the letters of thy name,
And o'er the number of thy years.

The mystic glory swims away;
 From off my bed the moonlight dies;
 And closing eaves of wearied eyes
I sleep till dusk is dipt in gray:

And then I know the mist is drawn
 A lucid veil from coast to coast,
 And in the dark church like a ghost
Thy tablet glimmers to the dawn.

LXVIII

When in the down I sink my head,
 Sleep, Death's twin-brother, times my breath;
 Sleep, Death's twin-brother, knows not Death,
Nor can I dream of thee as dead:

I walk as ere I walked forlorn,
 When all our path was fresh with dew,
 And all the bugle breezes blew
Reveillée to the breaking morn.

But what is this? I turn about,
  I find a trouble in thine eye,
   Which makes me sad I know not why,
Nor can my dream resolve the doubt:

But ere the lark hath left the lea
  I wake, and I discern the truth;
   It is the trouble of my youth
That foolish sleep transfers to thee.

LXIX

I dreamed there would be Spring no more,
  That Nature's ancient power was lost:
   The streets were black with smoke and frost,
They chattered trifles at the door:

I wandered from the noisy town,
  I found a wood with thorny boughs:
   I took the thorns to bind my brows,
I wore them like a civic crown:

I met with scoffs, I met with scorns
  From youth and babe and hoary hairs:
   They called me in the public squares
The fool that wears a crown of thorns:

They called me fool, they called me child:
  I found an angel of the night;
   The voice was low, the look was bright;
He looked upon my crown and smiled:

He reached the glory of a hand,
  That seemed to touch it into leaf:
   The voice was not the voice of grief,
The words were hard to understand.

LXX

I cannot see the features right,
    When on the gloom I strive to paint
    The face I know; the hues are faint
And mix with hollow masks of night;

Cloud-towers by ghostly masons wrought,
    A gulf that ever shuts and gapes,
    A hand that points, and pallèd shapes
In shadowy thoroughfares of thought;

And crowds that stream from yawning doors,
    And shoals of puckered faces drive;
    Dark bulks that tumble half alive,
And lazy lengths on boundless shores;

Till all at once beyond the will
    I hear a wizard music roll,
    And through a lattice on the soul
Looks thy fair face and makes it still.

LXXI

Sleep, kinsman thou to death and trance
    And madness, thou hast forged at last
    A night-long Present of the Past
In which we went through summer France.

Hadst thou such credit with the soul?
    Then bring an opiate trebly strong,
    Drug down the blindfold sense of wrong
That so my pleasure may be whole;

While now we talk as once we talked
  Of men and minds, the dust of change,
  The days that grow to something strange,
In walking as of old we walked

Beside the river's wooded reach,
  The fortress, and the mountain ridge,
  The cataract flashing from the bridge,
The breaker breaking on the beach.

LXXII

Risest thou thus, dim dawn, again,
  And howlest, issuing out of night,
  With blasts that blow the poplar white,
And lash with storm the streaming pane?

Day, when my crowned estate begun
  To pine in that reverse of doom,
  Which sickened every living bloom,
And blurred the splendour of the sun;

Who usherest in the dolorous hour
  With thy quick tears that make the rose
  Pull sideways, and the daisy close
Her crimson fringes to the shower;

Who might'st have heaved a windless flame
  Up the deep East, or, whispering, played
  A chequer-work of beam and shade
Along the hills, yet looked the same.

As wan, as chill, as wild as now;
  Day, marked as with some hideous crime,
  When the dark hand struck down through time,
And cancelled nature's best: but thou,

Lift as thou mayst thy burthened brows
   Through clouds that drench the morning star,
   And whirl the ungarnered sheaf afar,
And sow the sky with flying boughs,

And up thy vault with roaring sound
   Climb thy thick noon, disastrous day;
   Touch thy dull goal of joyless gray,
And hide thy shame beneath the ground.

LXXIII

So many worlds, so much to do,
   So little done, such things to be,
   How know I what had need of thee,
For thou wert strong as thou wert true?

The fame is quenched that I foresaw,
   The head hath missed an earthly wreath:
   I curse not nature, no, nor death;
For nothing is that errs from law.

We pass; the path that each man trod
   Is dim, or will be dim, with weeds:
   What fame is left for human deeds
In endless age? It rests with God.

O hollow wraith of dying fame,
   Fade wholly, while the soul exults,
   And self-infolds the large results
Of force that would have forged a name.

LXXIV

As sometimes in a dead man's face,
   To those that watch it more and more,
   A likeness, hardly seen before,
Comes out – to some one of his race:

So, dearest, now thy brows are cold,
   I see thee what thou art, and know
   Thy likeness to the wise below,
Thy kindred with the great of old.

But there is more than I can see,
   And what I see I leave unsaid,
   Nor speak it, knowing Death has made
His darkness beautiful with thee.

LXXV

I leave thy praises unexpressed
   In verse that brings myself relief,
   And by the measure of my grief
I leave thy greatness to be guessed;

What practice howsoe'er expert
   In fitting aptest words to things,
   Or voice the richest-toned that sings,
Hath power to give thee as thou wert?

I care not in these fading days
   To raise a cry that lasts not long,
   And round thee with the breeze of song
To stir a little dust of praise.

Thy leaf has perished in the green,
    And, while we breathe beneath the sun,
    The world which credits what is done
Is cold to all that might have been.

So here shall silence guard thy fame;
    But somewhere, out of human view,
    Whate'er thy hands are set to do
Is wrought with tumult of acclaim.

LXXVI

Take wings of fancy, and ascend,
    And in a moment set thy face
    Where all the starry heavens of space
Are sharpened to a needle's end;

Take wings of foresight; lighten through
    The secular abyss to come,
    And lo, thy deepest lays are dumb
Before the mouldering of a yew;

And if the matin songs, that woke
    The darkness of our planet, last,
    Thine own shall wither in the vast,
Ere half the lifetime of an oak.

Ere these have clothed their branchy bowers
    With fifty Mays, thy songs are vain;
    And what are they when these remain
The ruined shells of hollow towers?

LXXVII

What hope is here for modern rhyme
   To him, who turns a musing eye
   On songs, and deeds, and lives, that lie
Foreshortened in the tract of time?

These mortal lullabies of pain
   May bind a book, may line a box,
   May serve to curl a maiden's locks;
Or when a thousand moons shall wane

A man upon a stall may find,
   And, passing, turn the page that tells
   A grief, then changed to something else,
Sung by a long-forgotten mind.

But what of that? My darkened ways
   Shall ring with music all the same;
   To breathe my loss is more than fame,
To utter love more sweet than praise.

LXXVIII

Again at Christmas did we weave
   The holly round the Christmas hearth;
   The silent snow possessed the earth,
And calmly fell our Christmas-eve:

The yule-log sparkled keen with frost,
   No wing of wind the region swept,
   But over all things brooding slept
The quiet sense of something lost.

As in the winters left behind,
    Again our ancient games had place,
    The mimic picture's breathing grace,
And dance and song and hoodman-blind.

Who showed a token of distress?
    No single tear, no mark of pain:
    O sorrow, then can sorrow wane?
O grief, can grief be changed to less?

O last regret, regret can die!
    No – mixt with all this mystic frame,
    Her deep relations are the same,
But with long use her tears are dry.

LXXIX

'More than my brothers are to me,' –
    Let this not vex thee, noble heart!
    I know thee of what force thou art
To hold the costliest love in fee.

But thou and I are one in kind,
    As moulded like in Nature's mint;
    And hill and wood and field did print
The same sweet forms in either mind.

For us the same cold streamlet curled
    Through all his eddying coves; the same
    All winds that roam the twilight came
In whispers of the beauteous world.

At one dear knee we proffered vows,
    One lesson from one book we learned,
    Ere childhood's flaxen ringlet turned
To black and brown on kindred brows.

And so my wealth resembles thine,
 But he was rich where I was poor,
 And he supplied my want the more
As his unlikeness fitted mine.

LXXX

If any vague desire should rise,
 That holy Death ere Arthur died
 Had moved me kindly from his side,
And dropt the dust on tearless eyes;

Then fancy shapes, as fancy can,
 The grief my loss in him had wrought,
 A grief as deep as life or thought,
But stayed in peace with God and man.

I make a picture in the brain;
 I hear the sentence that he speaks;
 He bears the burthen of the weeks
But turns his burthen into gain.

His credit thus shall set me free;
 And, influence-rich to soothe and save,
 Unused example from the grave
Reach out dead hands to comfort me.

LXXXI

Could I have said while he was here,
 'My love shall now no further range;
 There cannot come a mellower change,
For now is love mature in ear.'

Love, then, had hope of richer store:
  What end is here to my complaint?
  This haunting whisper makes me faint,
'More years had made me love thee more.'

But Death returns an answer sweet:
  'My sudden frost was sudden gain,
  And gave all ripeness to the grain
It might have drawn from after-heat.'

LXXXII

I wage not any feud with Death
  For changes wrought on form and face;
  No lower life that earth's embrace
May breed with him, can fright my faith.

Eternal process moving on,
  From state to state the spirit walks;
  And these are but the shattered stalks,
Or ruined chrysalis of one.

Nor blame I Death, because he bare
  The use of virtue out of earth:
  I know transplanted human worth
Will bloom to profit, otherwhere.

For this alone on Death I wreak
  The wrath that garners in my heart;
  He put our lives so far apart
We cannot hear each other speak.

LXXXIII

Dip down upon the northern shore,
　　O sweet new-year delaying long;
　　Thou doest expectant nature wrong;
Delaying long, delay no more.

What stays thee from the clouded noons,
　　Thy sweetness from its proper place?
　　Can trouble live with April days,
Or sadness in the summer moons?

Bring orchis, bring the foxglove spire,
　　The little speedwell's darling blue,
　　Deep tulips dashed with fiery dew,
Laburnums, dropping-wells of fire.

O thou, new-year, delaying long,
　　Delayest the sorrow in my blood,
　　That longs to burst a frozen bud
And flood a fresher throat with song.

LXXXIV

When I contemplate all alone
　　The life that had been thine below,
　　And fix my thoughts on all the glow
To which thy crescent would have grown;

I see thee sitting crowned with good,
　　A central warmth diffusing bliss
　　In glance and smile, and clasp and kiss,
On all the branches of thy blood;

Thy blood, my friend, and partly mine;
   For now the day was drawing on,
   When thou shouldst link thy life with one
Of mine own house, and boys of thine

Had babbled 'Uncle' on my knee;
   But that remorseless iron hour
   Made cypress of her orange flower,
Despair of Hope, and earth of thee.

I seem to meet their least desire,
   To clap their cheeks, to call them mine.
   I see their unborn faces shine
Beside the never-lighted fire.

I see myself an honoured guest,
   Thy partner in the flowery walk
   Of letters, genial table-talk,
Or deep dispute, and graceful jest;

While now thy prosperous labour fills
   The lips of men with honest praise,
   And sun by sun the happy days
Descend below the golden hills

With promise of a morn as fair;
   And all the train of bounteous hours
   Conduct by paths of growing powers,
To reverence and the silver hair;

Till slowly worn her earthly robe,
   Her lavish mission richly wrought,
   Leaving great legacies of thought,
Thy spirit should fail from off the globe;

What time mine own might also flee,
 As linked with thine in love and fate,
 And, hovering o'er the dolorous strait
To the other shore, involved in thee,

Arrive at last the blessèd goal,
 And He that died in Holy Land
 Would reach us out the shining hand,
And take us as a single soul.

What reed was that on which I leant?
 Ah, backward fancy, wherefore wake
 The old bitterness again, and break
The low beginnings of content.

LXXXV

This truth came borne with bier and pall,
 I felt it, when I sorrowed most,
 'Tis better to have loved and lost,
Than never to have loved at all –

O true in word, and tried in deed,
 Demanding, so to bring relief
 To this which is our common grief,
What kind of life is that I lead;

And whether trust in things above
 Be dimmed of sorrow, or sustained;
 And whether love for him have drained
My capabilities of love;

Your words have virtue such as draws
 A faithful answer from the breast,
 Through light reproaches, half exprest,
And loyal unto kindly laws.

My blood an even tenor kept,
  Till on mine ear this message falls,
  That in Vienna's fatal walls
God's finger touched him, and he slept.

The great Intelligences fair
  That range above our mortal state,
  In circle round the blessèd gate,
Received and gave him welcome there;

And led him through the blissful climes,
  And showed him in the fountain fresh
  All knowledge that the sons of flesh
Shall gather in the cycled times.

But I remained, whose hopes were dim,
  Whose life, whose thoughts were little worth,
  To wander on a darkened earth,
Where all things round me breathed of him.

O friendship, equal-poised control,
  O heart, with kindliest motion warm,
  O sacred essence, other form,
O solemn ghost, O crownèd soul!

Yet none could better know than I,
  How much of act at human hands
  The sense of human will demands
By which we dare to live or die.

Whatever way my days decline,
  I felt and feel, though left alone,
  His being working in mine own,
The footsteps of his life in mine;

A life that all the Muses decked
    With gifts of grace, that might express
    All-comprehensive tenderness,
All-subtilising intellect:

And so my passion hath not swerved
    To works of weakness, but I find
    An image comforting the mind,
And in my grief a strength reserved.

Likewise the imaginative woe,
    That loved to handle spiritual strife,
    Diffused the shock through all my life,
But in the present broke the blow.

My pulses therefore beat again
    For other friends that once I met;
    Nor can it suit me to forget
The mighty hopes that make us men.

I woo your love: I count it crime
    To mourn for any overmuch;
    I, the divided half of such
A friendship as had mastered Time;

Which masters Time indeed, and is
    Eternal, separate from fears:
    The all-assuming months and years
Can take no part away from this:

But Summer on the steaming floods,
    And Spring that swells the narrow brooks,
    And Autumn, with a noise of rooks,
That gather in the waning woods,

And every pulse of wind and wave
   Recalls, in change of light or gloom,
   My old affection of the tomb,
And my prime passion in the grave:

My old affection of the tomb,
   A part of stillness, yearns to speak:
   'Arise, and get thee forth and seek
A friendship for the years to come.

'I watch thee from the quiet shore;
   Thy spirit up to mine can reach;
   But in dear words of human speech
We two communicate no more.'

And I, 'Can clouds of nature stain
   The starry clearness of the free?
   How is it? Canst thou feel for me
Some painless sympathy with pain?'

And lightly does the whisper fall;
   ''Tis hard for thee to fathom this;
   I triumph in conclusive bliss,
And that serene result of all.'

So hold I commerce with the dead;
   Or so methinks the dead would say;
   Or so shall grief with symbols play
And pining life be fancy-fed.

Now looking to some settled end,
   That these things pass, and I shall prove
   A meeting somewhere, love with love,
I crave your pardon, O my friend;

If not so fresh, with love as true,
 I, clasping brother-hands, aver
 I could not, if I would, transfer
The whole I felt for him to you.

For which be they that hold apart
 The promise of the golden hours?
 First love, first friendship, equal powers,
That marry with the virgin heart.

Still mine, that cannot but deplore,
 That beats within a lonely place,
 That yet remembers his embrace,
But at his footstep leaps no more,

My heart, though widowed, may not rest
 Quite in the love of what is gone,
 But seeks to beat in time with one
That warms another living breast.

Ah, take the imperfect gift I bring,
 Knowing the primrose yet is dear,
 The primrose of the later year,
As not unlike to that of Spring.

LXXXVI

Sweet after showers, ambrosial air,
 That rollest from the gorgeous gloom
 Of evening over brake and bloom
And meadow, slowly breathing bare

The round of space, and rapt below
 Through all the dewy-tasselled wood,
 And shadowing down the hornèd flood
In ripples, fan my brows and blow

The fever from my cheek, and sigh
   The full new life that feeds thy breath
   Throughout my frame, till Doubt and Death,
Ill brethren, let the fancy fly

From belt to belt of crimson seas
   On leagues of odour streaming far,
   To where in yonder orient star
A hundred spirits whisper 'Peace.'

LXXXVII

I past beside the reverend walls
   In which of old I wore the gown;
   I roved at random through the town,
And saw the tumult of the halls;

And heard once more in college fanes
   The storm their high-built organs make,
   And thunder-music, rolling, shake
The prophet blazoned on the panes;

And caught once more the distant shout,
   The measured pulse of racing oars
   Among the willows; paced the shores
And many a bridge, and all about

The same gray flats again, and felt
   The same, but not the same; and last
   Up that long walk of limes I past
To see the rooms in which he dwelt.

Another name was on the door:
   I lingered; all within was noise
   Of songs, and clapping hands, and boys
That crashed the glass and beat the floor;

Where once we held debate, a band
   Of youthful friends, on mind and art,
   And labour, and the changing mart,
And all the framework of the land;

When one would aim an arrow fair,
   But send it slackly from the string;
   And one would pierce an outer ring,
And one an inner, here and there;

And last the master-bowman, he,
   Would cleave the mark. A willing ear
   We lent him. Who, but hung to hear
The rapt oration flowing free

From point to point, with power and grace
   And music in the bounds of law,
   To those conclusions when we saw
The God within him light his face,

And seem to lift the form, and glow
   In azure orbits heavenly-wise;
   And over those ethereal eyes
The bar of Michael Angelo.

LXXXVIII

Wild bird, whose warble, liquid sweet,
   Rings Eden through the budded quicks,
   O tell me where the senses mix,
O tell me where the passions meet,

Whence radiate: fierce extremes employ
   Thy spirits in the darkening leaf,
   And in the midmost heart of grief
Thy passion clasps a secret joy:

And I – my harp would prelude woe –
    I cannot all command the strings;
    The glory of the sum of things
Will flash along the chords and go.

LXXXIX

Witch-elms that counterchange the floor
    Of this flat lawn with dusk and bright;
    And thou, with all thy breadth and height
Of foliage, towering sycamore;

How often, hither wandering down,
    My Arthur found your shadows fair,
    And shook to all the liberal air
The dust and din and steam of town:

He brought an eye for all he saw;
    He mixt in all our simple sports;
    They pleased him, fresh from brawling courts
And dusty purlieus of the law.

O joy to him in this retreat,
    Immantled in ambrosial dark,
    To drink the cooler air, and mark
The landscape winking through the heat:

O sound to rout the brood of cares,
    The sweep of scythe in morning dew,
    The gust that round the garden flew,
And tumbled half the mellowing pears!

O bliss, when all in circle drawn
    About him, heart and ear were fed
    To hear him, as he lay and read
The Tuscan poets on the lawn:

Or in the all-golden afternoon
  A guest, or happy sister, sung,
  Or here she brought the harp and flung
A ballad to the brightening moon:

Nor less it pleased in livelier moods,
  Beyond the bounding hill to stray,
  And break the livelong summer day
With banquet in the distant woods;

Whereat we glanced from theme to theme,
  Discussed the books to love or hate,
  Or touched the changes of the state,
Or threaded some Socratic dream;

But if I praised the busy town,
  He loved to rail against it still,
  For 'ground in yonder social mill
We rub each other's angles down,

'And merge' he said 'in form and gloss
  The picturesque of man and man.'
  We talked: the stream beneath us ran,
The wine-flask lying couched in moss,

Or cooled within the glooming wave;
  And last, returning from afar,
  Before the crimson-circled star
Had fallen into her father's grave,

And brushing ankle-deep in flowers,
  We heard behind the woodbine veil
  The milk that bubbled in the pail,
And buzzings of the honied hours.

XC

He tasted love with half his mind,
   Nor ever drank the inviolate spring
   Where nighest heaven, who first could fling
This bitter seed among mankind;

That could the dead, whose dying eyes
   Were closed with wail, resume their life,
   They would but find in child and wife
An iron welcome when they rise:

'Twas well, indeed, when warm with wine,
   To pledge them with a kindly tear,
   To talk them o'er, to wish them here,
To count their memories half divine;

But if they came who past away,
   Behold their brides in other hands;
   The hard heir strides about their lands,
And will not yield them for a day.

Yea, though their sons were none of these,
   Not less the yet-loved sire would make
   Confusion worse than death, and shake
The pillars of domestic peace.

Ah dear, but come thou back to me:
   Whatever change the years have wrought,
   I find not yet one lonely thought
That cries against my wish for thee.

XCI

When rosy plumelets tuft the larch,
   And rarely pipes the mounted thrush;
   Or underneath the barren bush
Flits by the sea-blue bird of March;

Come, wear the form by which I know
   Thy spirit in time among thy peers;
   The hope of unaccomplished years
Be large and lucid round thy brow.

When summer's hourly-mellowing change
   May breathe, with many roses sweet,
   Upon the thousand waves of wheat,
That ripple round the lonely grange;

Come: not in watches of the night,
   But where the sunbeam broodeth warm,
   Come, beauteous in thine after form,
And like a finer light in light.

XCII

If any vision should reveal
   Thy likeness, I might count it vain
   As but the canker of the brain;
Yea, though it spake and made appeal

To chances where our lots were cast
   Together in the days behind,
   I might but say, I hear a wind
Of memory murmuring the past.

Yea, though it spake and bared to view
  A fact within the coming year;
  And though the months, revolving near,
Should prove the phantom-warning true,

They might not seem thy prophecies,
  But spiritual presentiments,
  And such refraction of events
As often rises ere they rise.

XCIII

I shall not see thee. Dare I say
  No spirit ever brake the band
  That stays him from the native land
Where first he walked when claspt in clay?

No visual shade of some one lost,
  But he, the Spirit himself, may come
  Where all the nerve of sense is numb;
Spirit to Spirit, Ghost to Ghost.

O, therefore from thy sightless range
  With gods in unconjectured bliss,
  O, from the distance of the abyss
Of tenfold-complicated change,

Descend, and touch, and enter; hear
  The wish too strong for words to name;
  That in this blindness of the frame
My Ghost may feel that thine is near.

XCIV

How pure at heart and sound in head,
   With what divine affections bold
   Should be the man whose thought would hold
An hour's communion with the dead.

In vain shalt thou, or any, call
   The spirits from their golden day,
   Except, like them, thou too canst say,
My spirit is at peace with all.

They haunt the silence of the breast,
   Imaginations calm and fair,
   The memory like a cloudless air,
The conscience as a sea at rest:

But when the heart is full of din,
   And doubt beside the portal waits,
   They can but listen at the gates,
And hear the household jar within.

XCV

By night we lingered on the lawn,
   For underfoot the herb was dry;
   And genial warmth; and o'er the sky
The silvery haze of summer drawn;

And calm that let the tapers burn
   Unwavering: not a cricket chirred:
   The brook alone far-off was heard,
And on the board the fluttering urn:

And bats went round in fragrant skies,
  And wheeled or lit the filmy shapes
  That haunt the dusk, with ermine capes
And woolly breasts and beaded eyes;

While now we sang old songs that pealed
  From knoll to knoll, where, couched at ease,
  The white kine glimmered, and the trees
Laid their dark arms about the field.

But when those others, one by one,
  Withdrew themselves from me and night,
  And in the house light after light
Went out, and I was all alone,

A hunger seized my heart; I read
  Of that glad year which once had been,
  In those fallen leaves which kept their green,
The noble letters of the dead:

And strangely on the silence broke
  The silent-speaking words, and strange
  Was love's dumb cry defying change
To test his worth; and strangely spoke

The faith, the vigour, bold to dwell
  On doubts that drive the coward back,
  And keen through wordy snares to track
Suggestion to her inmost cell.

So word by word, and line by line,
  The dead man touched me from the past,
  And all at once it seemed at last
The living soul was flashed on mine,

And mine in this was wound, and whirled
   About empyreal heights of thought,
   And came on that which is, and caught
The deep pulsations of the world,

Æonian music measuring out
   The steps of Time – the shocks of Chance –
   The blows of Death. At length my trance
Was cancelled, stricken through with doubt.

Vague words! but ah, how hard to frame
   In matter-moulded forms of speech,
   Or even for intellect to reach
Through memory that which I became:

Till now the doubtful dusk revealed
   The knolls once more where, couched at ease,
   The white kine glimmered, and the trees
Laid their dark arms about the field:

And sucked from out the distant gloom
   A breeze began to tremble o'er
   The large leaves of the sycamore,
And fluctuate all the still perfume,

And gathering freshlier overhead,
   Rocked the full-foliaged elms, and swung
   The heavy-folded rose, and flung
The lilies to and fro, and said,

'The dawn, the dawn,' and died away;
   And East and West, without a breath,
   Mixt their dim lights, like life and death,
To broaden into boundless day.

XCVI

You say, but with no touch of scorn,
　　Sweet-hearted, you, whose light-blue eyes
　　Are tender over drowning flies,
You tell me, doubt is Devil-born.

I know not: one indeed I knew
　　In many a subtle question versed,
　　Who touched a jarring lyre at first,
But ever strove to make it true:

Perplext in faith, but pure in deeds,
　　At last he beat his music out.
　　There lives more faith in honest doubt,
Believe me, than in half the creeds.

He fought his doubts and gathered strength,
　　He would not make his judgment blind,
　　He faced the spectres of the mind
And laid them: thus he came at length

To find a stronger faith his own;
　　And Power was with him in the night,
　　Which makes the darkness and the light,
And dwells not in the light alone,

But in the darkness and the cloud,
　　As over Sinaï's peaks of old,
　　While Israel made their gods of gold,
Although the trumpet blew so loud.

XCVII

My love has talked with rocks and trees;
   He finds on misty mountain-ground
   His own vast shadow glory-crowned;
He sees himself in all he sees.

Two partners of a married life –
   I looked on these and thought of thee
   In vastness and in mystery,
And of my spirit as of a wife.

These two – they dwelt with eye on eye,
   Their hearts of old have beat in tune,
   Their meetings made December June,
Their every parting was to die.

Their love has never past away;
   The days she never can forget
   Are earnest that he loves her yet,
Whate'er the faithless people say.

Her life is lone, he sits apart,
   He loves her yet, she will not weep,
   Though rapt in matters dark and deep
He seems to slight her simple heart.

He thrids the labyrinth of the mind,
   He reads the secret of the star,
   He seems so near and yet so far,
He looks so cold: she thinks him kind.

She keeps the gift of years before,
   A withered violet is her bliss:
   She knows not what his greatness is,
For that, for all, she loves him more.

For him she plays, to him she sings
  Of early faith and plighted vows;
   She knows but matters of the house,
And he, he knows a thousand things.

Her faith is fixt and cannot move,
  She darkly feels him great and wise,
   She dwells on him with faithful eyes,
'I cannot understand: I love.'

XCVIII

You leave us: you will see the Rhine,
  And those fair hills I sailed below,
   When I was there with him; and go
By summer belts of wheat and vine

To where he breathed his latest breath,
  That City. All her splendour seems
   No livelier than the wisp that gleams
On Lethe in the eyes of Death.

Let her great Danube rolling fair
  Enwind her isles, unmarked of me:
   I have not seen, I will not see
Vienna; rather dream that there,

A treble darkness, Evil haunts
  The birth, the bridal; friend from friend
   Is oftener parted, fathers bend
Above more graves, a thousand wants

Gnarr at the heels of men, and prey
  By each cold hearth, and sadness flings
   Her shadow on the blaze of kings:
And yet myself have heard him say,

That not in any mother town
   With statelier progress to and fro
   The double tides of chariots flow
By park and suburb under brown

Of lustier leaves; nor more content,
   He told me, lives in any crowd,
   When all is gay with lamps, and loud
With sport and song, in booth and tent,

Imperial halls, or open plain;
   And wheels the circled dance, and breaks
   The rocket molten into flakes
Of crimson or in emerald rain.

XCIX

Risest thou thus, dim dawn, again,
   So loud with voices of the birds,
   So thick with lowings of the herds,
Day, when I lost the flower of men;

Who tremblest through thy darkling red
   On yon swollen brook that bubbles fast
   By meadows breathing of the past,
And woodlands holy to the dead;

Who murmurest in the foliaged eaves
   A song that slights the coming care,
   And Autumn laying here and there
A fiery finger on the leaves;

Who wakenest with thy balmy breath
   To myriads on the genial earth,
   Memories of bridal, or of birth,
And unto myriads more, of death.

O wheresoever those may be,
   Betwixt the slumber of the poles,
   Today they count as kindred souls;
They know me not, but mourn with me.

C

I climb the hill: from end to end
   Of all the landscape underneath,
   I find no place that does not breathe
Some gracious memory of my friend;

No gray old grange, or lonely fold,
   Or low morass and whispering reed,
   Or simple stile from mead to mead,
Or sheepwalk up the windy wold;

Nor hoary knoll of ash and haw
   That hears the latest linnet trill,
   Nor quarry trenched along the hill
And haunted by the wrangling daw;

Nor runlet tinkling from the rock;
   Nor pastoral rivulet that swerves
   To left and right through meadowy curves,
That feed the mothers of the flock;

But each has pleased a kindred eye,
   And each reflects a kindlier day;
   And, leaving these, to pass away,
I think once more he seems to die.

CI

Unwatched, the garden bough shall sway,
  The tender blossom flutter down,
  Unloved, that beech will gather brown,
This maple burn itself away;

Unloved, the sun-flower, shining fair,
  Ray round with flames her disk of seed,
  And many a rose-carnation feed
With summer spice the humming air;

Unloved, by many a sandy bar,
  The brook shall babble down the plain,
  At noon or when the lesser wain
Is twisting round the polar star;

Uncared for, gird the windy grove,
  And flood the haunts of hern and crake;
  Or into silver arrows break
The sailing moon in creek and cove;

Till from the garden and the wild
  A fresh association blow,
  And year by year the landscape grow
Familiar to the stranger's child;

As year by year the labourer tills
  His wonted glebe, or lops the glades;
  And year by year our memory fades
From all the circle of the hills.

CII

We leave the well-belovèd place
 Where first we gazed upon the sky;
 The roofs, that heard our earliest cry,
Will shelter one of stranger race.

We go, but ere we go from home,
 As down the garden-walks I move,
 Two spirits of a diverse love
Contend for loving masterdom.

One whispers, 'Here thy boyhood sung
 Long since its matin song, and heard
 The low love-language of the bird
In native hazels tassel-hung.'

The other answers, 'Yea, but here
 Thy feet have strayed in after hours
 With thy lost friend among the bowers,
And this hath made them trebly dear.'

These two have striven half the day,
 And each prefers his separate claim,
 Poor rivals in a losing game,
That will not yield each other way.

I turn to go: my feet are set
 To leave the pleasant fields and farms;
 They mix in one another's arms
To one pure image of regret.

CIII

On that last night before we went
    From out the doors where I was bred,
    I dreamed a vision of the dead,
Which left my after-morn content.

Methought I dwelt within a hall,
    And maidens with me: distant hills
    From hidden summits fed with rills
A river sliding by the wall.

The hall with harp and carol rang.
    They sang of what is wise and good
    And graceful. In the centre stood
A statue veiled, to which they sang;

And which, though veiled, was known to me,
    The shape of him I loved, and love
    For ever: then flew in a dove
And brought a summons from the sea:

And when they learnt that I must go
    They wept and wailed, but led the way
    To where a little shallop lay
At anchor in the flood below;

And on by many a level mead,
    And shadowing bluff that made the banks,
    We glided winding under ranks
Of iris, and the golden reed;

And still as vaster grew the shore
    And rolled the floods in grander space,
    The maidens gathered strength and grace
And presence, lordlier than before;

And I myself, who sat apart
   And watched them, waxed in every limb;
   I felt the thews of Anakim,
The pulses of a Titan's heart;

As one would sing the death of war,
   And one would chant the history
   Of that great race, which is to be,
And one the shaping of a star;

Until the forward-creeping tides
   Began to foam, and we to draw
   From deep to deep, to where we saw
A great ship lift her shining sides.

The man we loved was there on deck,
   But thrice as large as man he bent
   To greet us. Up the side I went,
And fell in silence on his neck:

Whereat those maidens with one mind
   Bewailed their lot; I did them wrong:
   'We served thee here,' they said, 'so long,
And wilt thou leave us now behind?'

So rapt I was, they could not win
   An answer from my lips, but he
   Replying, 'Enter likewise ye
And go with us:' they entered in.

And while the wind began to sweep
   A music out of sheet and shroud,
   We steered her toward a crimson cloud
That landlike slept along the deep.

CIV

The time draws near the birth of Christ;
   The moon is hid, the night is still;
   A single church below the hill
Is pealing, folded in the mist.

A single peal of bells below,
   That wakens at this hour of rest
   A single murmur in the breast,
That these are not the bells I know.

Like strangers' voices here they sound,
   In lands where not a memory strays,
   Nor landmark breathes of other days,
But all is new unhallowed ground.

CV

Tonight ungathered let us leave
   This laurel, let this holly stand:
   We live within the stranger's land,
And strangely falls our Christmas-eve.

Our father's dust is left alone
   And silent under other snows:
   There in due time the woodbine blows,
The violet comes, but we are gone.

No more shall wayward grief abuse
   The genial hour with mask and mime;
   For change of place, like growth of time,
Has broke the bond of dying use.

Let cares that petty shadows cast,
   By which our lives are chiefly proved,
   A little spare the night I loved,
And hold it solemn to the past.

But let no footstep beat the floor,
   Nor bowl of wassail mantle warm;
   For who would keep an ancient form
Through which the spirit breathes no more?

Be neither song, nor game, nor feast;
   Nor harp be touched, nor flute be blown;
   No dance, no motion, save alone
What lightens in the lucid east

Of rising worlds by yonder wood.
   Long sleeps the summer in the seed;
   Run out your measured arcs, and lead
The closing cycle rich in good.

CVI

Ring out, wild bells, to the wild sky,
   The flying cloud, the frosty light:
   The year is dying in the night;
Ring out, wild bells, and let him die.

Ring out the old, ring in the new,
   Ring, happy bells, across the snow:
   The year is going, let him go;
Ring out the false, ring in the true.

Ring out the grief that saps the mind,
   For those that here we see no more;
   Ring out the feud of rich and poor,
Ring in redress to all mankind.

Ring out a slowly dying cause,
 And ancient forms of party strife;
 Ring in the nobler modes of life,
With sweeter manners, purer laws.

Ring out the want, the care, the sin,
 The faithless coldness of the times;
 Ring out, ring out my mournful rhymes,
But ring the fuller minstrel in.

Ring out false pride in place and blood,
 The civic slander and the spite;
 Ring in the love of truth and right,
Ring in the common love of good.

Ring out old shapes of foul disease;
 Ring out the narrowing lust of gold;
 Ring out the thousand wars of old,
Ring in the thousand years of peace.

Ring in the valiant man and free,
 The larger heart, the kindlier hand;
 Ring out the darkness of the land,
Ring in the Christ that is to be.

CVII

It is the day when he was born,
 A bitter day that early sank
 Behind a purple-frosty bank
Of vapour, leaving night forlorn.

The time admits not flowers or leaves
 To deck the banquet. Fiercely flies
 The blast of North and East, and ice
Makes daggers at the sharpened eaves,

And bristles all the brakes and thorns
  To yon hard crescent, as she hangs
  Above the wood which grides and clangs
Its leafless ribs and iron horns

Together, in the drifts that pass
  To darken on the rolling brine
  That breaks the coast. But fetch the wine,
Arrange the board and brim the glass;

Bring in great logs and let them lie,
  To make a solid core of heat;
  Be cheerful-minded, talk and treat
Of all things even as he were by;

We keep the day. With festal cheer,
  With books and music, surely we
  Will drink to him, whate'er he be,
And sing the songs he loved to hear.

CVIII

I will not shut me from my kind,
  And, lest I stiffen into stone,
  I will not eat my heart alone,
Nor feed with sighs a passing wind:

What profit lies in barren faith,
  And vacant yearning, though with might
  To scale the heaven's highest height,
Or dive below the wells of Death?

What find I in the highest place,
  But mine own phantom chanting hymns?
  And on the depths of death there swims
The reflex of a human face.

I'll rather take what fruit may be
  Of sorrow under human skies:
  'Tis held that sorrow makes us wise,
Whatever wisdom sleep with thee.

CIX

Heart-affluence in discursive talk
  From household fountains never dry;
  The critic clearness of an eye,
That saw through all the Muses' walk;

Seraphic intellect and force
  To seize and throw the doubts of man;
  Impassioned logic, which outran
The hearer in its fiery course;

High nature amorous of the good,
  But touched with no ascetic gloom;
  And passion pure in snowy bloom
Through all the years of April blood;

A love of freedom rarely felt,
  Of freedom in her regal seat
  Of England; not the schoolboy heat,
The blind hysterics of the Celt;

And manhood fused with female grace
  In such a sort, the child would twine
  A trustful hand, unasked, in thine,
And find his comfort in thy face;

All these have been, and thee mine eyes
  Have looked on: if they looked in vain,
  My shame is greater who remain,
Nor let thy wisdom make me wise.

CX

Thy converse drew us with delight,
   The men of rathe and riper years:
   The feeble soul, a haunt of fears,
Forgot his weakness in thy sight.

On thee the loyal-hearted hung,
   The proud was half disarmed of pride,
   Nor cared the serpent at thy side
To flicker with his double tongue.

The stern were mild when thou wert by,
   The flippant put himself to school
   And heard thee, and the brazen fool
Was softened, and he knew not why;

While I, thy nearest, sat apart,
   And felt thy triumph was as mine;
   And loved them more, that they were thine,
The graceful tact, the Christian art;

Nor mine the sweetness or the skill,
   But mine the love that will not tire,
   And, born of love, the vague desire
That spurs an imitative will.

CXI

The churl in spirit, up or down
   Along the scale of ranks, through all,
   To him who grasps a golden ball,
By blood a king, at heart a clown;

The churl in spirit, howe'er he veil
   His want in forms for fashion's sake,
   Will let his coltish nature break
At seasons through the gilded pale:

For who can always act? but he,
   To whom a thousand memories call,
   Not being less but more than all
The gentleness he seemed to be,

Best seemed the thing he was, and joined
   Each office of the social hour
   To noble manners, as the flower
And native growth of noble mind;

Nor ever narrowness or spite,
   Or villain fancy fleeting by,
   Drew in the expression of an eye,
Where God and Nature met in light;

And thus he bore without abuse
   The grand old name of gentleman,
   Defamed by every charlatan,
And soiled with all ignoble use.

CXII

High wisdom holds my wisdom less,
   That I, who gaze with temperate eyes
   On glorious insufficiencies,
Set light by narrower perfectness.

But thou, that fillest all the room
   Of all my love, art reason why
   I seem to cast a careless eye
On souls, the lesser lords of doom.

For what wert thou? some novel power
   Sprang up for ever at a touch,
   And hope could never hope too much,
In watching thee from hour to hour,

Large elements in order brought,
   And tracts of calm from tempest made,
   And world-wide fluctuation swayed
In vassal tides that followed thought.

CXIII

'Tis held that sorrow makes us wise;
   Yet how much wisdom sleeps with thee
   Which not alone had guided me,
But served the seasons that may rise;

For can I doubt, who knew thee keen
   In intellect, with force and skill
   To strive, to fashion, to fulfil –
I doubt not what thou wouldst have been:

A life in civic action warm,
   A soul on highest mission sent,
   A potent voice of Parliament,
A pillar steadfast in the storm,

Should licensed boldness gather force,
   Becoming, when the time has birth,
   A lever to uplift the earth
And roll it in another course,

With thousand shocks that come and go,
   With agonies, with energies,
   With overthrowings, and with cries,
And undulations to and fro.

CXIV

Who loves not Knowledge? Who shall rail
   Against her beauty? May she mix
   With men and prosper! Who shall fix
Her pillars? Let her work prevail.

But on her forehead sits a fire:
   She sets her forward countenance
   And leaps into the future chance,
Submitting all things to desire.

Half-grown as yet, a child, and vain –
   She cannot fight the fear of death.
   What is she, cut from love and faith,
But some wild Pallas from the brain

Of Demons? fiery-hot to burst
   All barriers in her onward race
   For power. Let her know her place;
She is the second, not the first.

A higher hand must make her mild,
   If all be not in vain; and guide
   Her footsteps, moving side by side
With wisdom, like the younger child:

For she is earthly of the mind,
   But Wisdom heavenly of the soul.
   O, friend, who camest to thy goal
So early, leaving me behind,

I would the great world grew like thee,
   Who grewest not alone in power
   And knowledge, but by year and hour
In reverence and in charity.

CXV

Now fades the last long streak of snow,
   Now burgeons every maze of quick
   About the flowering squares, and thick
By ashen roots the violets blow.

Now rings the woodland loud and long,
   The distance takes a lovelier hue,
   And drowned in yonder living blue
The lark becomes a sightless song.

Now dance the lights on lawn and lea,
   The flocks are whiter down the vale,
   And milkier every milky sail
On winding stream or distant sea;

Where now the seamew pipes, or dives
   In yonder greening gleam, and fly
   The happy birds, that change their sky
To build and brood; that live their lives

From land to land; and in my breast
   Spring wakens too; and my regret
   Becomes an April violet,
And buds and blossoms like the rest.

CXVI

Is it, then, regret for buried time
   That keenlier in sweet April wakes,
   And meets the year, and gives and takes
The colours of the crescent prime?

Not all: the songs, the stirring air,
  The life re-orient out of dust,
  Cry through the sense to hearten trust
In that which made the world so fair.

Not all regret: the face will shine
  Upon me, while I muse alone;
  And that dear voice, I once have known,
Still speak to me of me and mine:

Yet less of sorrow lives in me
  For days of happy commune dead;
  Less yearning for the friendship fled,
Than some strong bond which is to be.

CXVII

O days and hours, your work is this,
  To hold me from my proper place,
  A little while from his embrace,
For fuller gain of after bliss:

That out of distance might ensue
  Desire of nearness doubly sweet;
  And unto meeting when we meet,
Delight a hundredfold accrue,

For every grain of sand that runs,
  And every span of shade that steals,
  And every kiss of toothèd wheels,
And all the courses of the suns.

CXVIII

Contemplate all this work of Time,
  The giant labouring in his youth;
  Nor dream of human love and truth,
As dying Nature's earth and lime;

But trust that those we call the dead
  Are breathers of an ampler day
  For ever nobler ends. They say,
The solid earth whereon we tread

In tracts of fluent heat began,
  And grew to seeming-random forms,
  The seeming prey of cyclic storms,
Till at the last arose the man;

Who throve and branched from clime to clime,
  The herald of a higher race,
  And of himself in higher place,
If so he type this work of time

Within himself, from more to more;
  Or, crowned with attributes of woe
  Like glories, move his course, and show
That life is not as idle ore,

But iron dug from central gloom,
  And heated hot with burning fears,
  And dipt in baths of hissing tears,
And battered with the shocks of doom

To shape and use. Arise and fly
  The reeling Faun, the sensual feast;
  Move upward, working out the beast,
And let the ape and tiger die.

CXIX

Doors, where my heart was used to beat
    So quickly, not as one that weeps
    I come once more; the city sleeps;
I smell the meadow in the street;

I hear a chirp of birds; I see
    Betwixt the black fronts long-withdrawn
    A light-blue lane of early dawn,
And think of early days and thee,

And bless thee, for thy lips are bland,
    And bright the friendship of thine eye;
    And in my thoughts with scarce a sigh
I take the pressure of thine hand.

CXX

I trust I have not wasted breath:
    I think we are not wholly brain,
    Magnetic mockeries; not in vain,
Like Paul with beasts, I fought with Death;

Not only cunning casts in clay:
    Let Science prove we are, and then
    What matters Science unto men,
At least to me? I would not stay.

Let him, the wiser man who springs
    Hereafter, up from childhood shape
    His action like the greater ape,
But I was *born* to other things.

CXXI

Sad Hesper o'er the buried sun
  And ready, thou, to die with him,
  Thou watchest all things ever dim
And dimmer, and a glory done:

The team is loosened from the wain,
  The boat is drawn upon the shore;
  Thou listenest to the closing door,
And life is darkened in the brain.

Bright Phosphor, fresher for the night,
  By thee the world's great work is heard
  Beginning, and the wakeful bird;
Behind thee comes the greater light:

The market boat is on the stream,
  And voices hail it from the brink;
  Thou hear'st the village hammer clink,
And see'st the moving of the team.

Sweet Hesper-Phosphor, double name
  For what is one, the first, the last,
  Thou, like my present and my past,
Thy place is changed; thou art the same.

CXXII

Oh, wast thou with me, dearest, then,
  While I rose up against my doom,
  And yearned to burst the folded gloom,
To bare the eternal Heavens again,

To feel once more, in placid awe,
  The strong imagination roll
  A sphere of stars about my soul,
In all her motion one with law;

If thou wert with me, and the grave
  Divide us not, be with me now,
  And enter in at breast and brow,
Till all my blood, a fuller wave,

Be quickened with a livelier breath,
  And like an inconsiderate boy,
  As in the former flash of joy,
I slip the thoughts of life and death;

And all the breeze of Fancy blows,
  And every dew-drop paints a bow,
  The wizard lightnings deeply glow,
And every thought breaks out a rose.

CXXIII

There rolls the deep where grew the tree.
  O earth, what changes hast thou seen!
  There where the long street roars, hath been
The stillness of the central sea.

The hills are shadows, and they flow
  From form to form, and nothing stands;
  They melt like mist, the solid lands,
Like clouds they shape themselves and go.

But in my spirit will I dwell,
  And dream my dream, and hold it true;
  For though my lips may breathe adieu,
I cannot think the thing farewell.

CXXIV

That which we dare invoke to bless;
  Our dearest faith; our ghastliest doubt;
  He, They, One, All; within, without;
The Power in darkness whom we guess;

I found Him not in world or sun,
  Or eagle's wing, or insect's eye;
  Nor through the questions men may try,
The petty cobwebs we have spun:

If e'er when faith had fallen asleep,
  I heard a voice 'believe no more'
  And heard an ever-breaking shore
That tumbled in the Godless deep;

A warmth within the breast would melt
  The freezing reason's colder part,
  And like a man in wrath the heart
Stood up and answered 'I have felt.'

No, like a child in doubt and fear:
  But that blind clamour made me wise;
  Then was I as a child that cries,
But, crying, knows his father near;

And what I am beheld again
  What is, and no man understands;
  And out of darkness came the hands
That reach through nature, moulding men.

CXXV

Whatever I have said or sung,
   Some bitter notes my harp would give,
   Yea, though there often seemed to live
A contradiction on the tongue,

Yet Hope had never lost her youth;
   She did but look through dimmer eyes;
   Or Love but played with gracious lies,
Because he felt so fixed in truth:

And if the song were full of care,
   He breathed the spirit of the song;
   And if the words were sweet and strong
He set his royal signet there;

Abiding with me till I sail
   To seek thee on the mystic deeps,
   And this electric force, that keeps
A thousand pulses dancing, fail.

CXXVI

Love is and was my Lord and King,
   And in his presence I attend
   To hear the tidings of my friend,
Which every hour his couriers bring.

Love is and was my King and Lord,
   And will be, though as yet I keep
   Within his court on earth, and sleep
Encompassed by his faithful guard,

And hear at times a sentinel
  Who moves about from place to place,
  And whispers to the worlds of space,
In the deep night, that all is well.

CXXVII

And all is well, though faith and form
  Be sundered in the night of fear;
  Well roars the storm to those that hear
A deeper voice across the storm,

Proclaiming social truth shall spread,
  And justice, even though thrice again
  The red fool-fury of the Seine
Should pile her barricades with dead.

But ill for him that wears a crown,
  And him, the lazar, in his rags:
  They tremble, the sustaining crags;
The spires of ice are toppled down,

And molten up, and roar in flood;
  The fortress crashes from on high,
  The brute earth lightens to the sky,
And the great Æon sinks in blood,

And compassed by the fires of Hell;
  While thou, dear spirit, happy star,
  O'erlook'st the tumult from afar,
And smilest, knowing all is well.

CXXVIII

The love that rose on stronger wings,
    Unpalsied when he met with Death,
    Is comrade of the lesser faith
That sees the course of human things.

No doubt vast eddies in the flood
    Of onward time shall yet be made,
    And thronèd races may degrade;
Yet O ye mysteries of good,

Wild Hours that fly with Hope and Fear,
    If all your office had to do
    With old results that look like new;
If this were all your mission here,

To draw, to sheathe a useless sword,
    To fool the crowd with glorious lies,
    To cleave a creed in sects and cries,
To change the bearing of a word,

To shift an arbitrary power,
    To cramp the student at his desk,
    To make old bareness picturesque
And tuft with grass a feudal tower;

Why then my scorn might well descend
    On you and yours. I see in part
    That all, as in some piece of art,
Is toil cöoperant to an end.

CXXIX

Dear friend, far off, my lost desire,
  So far, so near in woe and weal;
  O loved the most, when most I feel
There is a lower and a higher;

Known and unknown; human, divine;
  Sweet human hand and lips and eye;
  Dear heavenly friend that canst not die,
Mine, mine, for ever, ever mine;

Strange friend, past, present, and to be;
  Loved deeplier, darklier understood;
  Behold, I dream a dream of good,
And mingle all the world with thee.

CXXX

Thy voice is on the rolling air;
  I hear thee where the waters run;
  Thou standest in the rising sun,
And in the setting thou art fair.

What art thou then? I cannot guess;
  But though I seem in star and flower
  To feel thee some diffusive power,
I do not therefore love thee less:

My love involves the love before;
  My love is vaster passion now;
  Though mixed with God and Nature thou,
I seem to love thee more and more.

Far off thou art, but ever nigh;
   I have thee still, and I rejoice;
   I prosper, circled with thy voice;
I shall not lose thee though I die.

CXXXI

O living will that shalt endure
   When all that seems shall suffer shock,
   Rise in the spiritual rock,
Flow through our deeds and make them pure,

That we may lift from out of dust
   A voice as unto him that hears,
   A cry above the conquered years
To one that with us works, and trust,

With faith that comes of self-control,
   The truths that never can be proved
   Until we close with all we loved,
And all we flow from, soul in soul.

EPILOGUE

O true and tried, so well and long,
   Demand not thou a marriage lay;
   In that it is thy marriage day
Is music more than any song.

Nor have I felt so much of bliss
   Since first he told me that he loved
   A daughter of our house; nor proved
Since that dark day a day like this;

Though I since then have numbered o'er
    Some thrice three years: they went and came,
    Remade the blood and changed the frame,
And yet is love not less, but more;

No longer caring to embalm
    In dying songs a dead regret,
    But like a statue solid-set,
And moulded in colossal calm.

Regret is dead, but love is more
    Than in the summers that are flown,
    For I myself with these have grown
To something greater than before;

Which makes appear the songs I made
    As echoes out of weaker times,
    As half but idle brawling rhymes,
The sport of random sun and shade.

But where is she, the bridal flower,
    That must be made a wife ere noon?
    She enters, glowing like the moon
Of Eden on its bridal bower:

On me she bends her blissful eyes
    And then on thee; they meet thy look
    And brighten like the star that shook
Betwixt the palms of paradise.

O when her life was yet in bud,
    He too foretold the perfect rose.
    For thee she grew, for thee she grows
For ever, and as fair as good.

And thou art worthy; full of power;
   As gentle; liberal-minded, great,
   Consistent; wearing all that weight
Of learning lightly like a flower.

But now set out: the noon is near,
   And I must give away the bride;
   She fears not, or with thee beside
And me behind her, will not fear.

For I that danced her on my knee,
   That watched her on her nurse's arm,
   That shielded all her life from harm
At last must part with her to thee;

Now waiting to be made a wife,
   Her feet, my darling, on the dead;
   Their pensive tablets round her head,
And the most living words of life

Breathed in her ear. The ring is on,
   The 'wilt thou' answered, and again
   The 'wilt thou' asked, till out of twain
Her sweet 'I will' has made you one.

Now sign your names, which shall be read,
   Mute symbols of a joyful morn,
   By village eyes as yet unborn;
The names are signed, and overhead

Begins the clash and clang that tells
   The joy to every wandering breeze;
   The blind wall rocks, and on the trees
The dead leaf trembles to the bells.

O happy hour, and happier hours
   Await them. Many a merry face
   Salutes them – maidens of the place,
That pelt us in the porch with flowers.

O happy hour, behold the bride
   With him to whom her hand I gave.
   They leave the porch, they pass the grave
That has today its sunny side.

Today the grave is bright for me,
   For them the light of life increased,
   Who stay to share the morning feast,
Who rest tonight beside the sea.

Let all my genial spirits advance
   To meet and greet a whiter sun;
   My drooping memory will not shun
The foaming grape of eastern France.

It circles round, and fancy plays,
   And hearts are warmed and faces bloom,
   As drinking health to bride and groom
We wish them store of happy days.

Nor count me all to blame if I
   Conjecture of a stiller guest,
   Perchance, perchance, among the rest,
And, though in silence, wishing joy.

But they must go, the time draws on,
   And those white-favoured horses wait;
   They rise, but linger; it is late;
Farewell, we kiss, and they are gone.

A shade falls on us like the dark
   From little cloudlets on the grass,
   But sweeps away as out we pass
To range the woods, to roam the park,

Discussing how their courtship grew,
   And talk of others that are wed,
   And how she looked, and what he said,
And back we come at fall of dew.

Again the feast, the speech, the glee,
   The shade of passing thought, the wealth
   Of words and wit, the double health,
The crowning cup, the three-times-three,

And last the dance; – till I retire:
   Dumb is that tower which spake so loud,
   And high in heaven the streaming cloud,
And on the downs a rising fire:

And rise, O moon, from yonder down,
   Till over down and over dale
   All night the shining vapour sail
And pass the silent-lighted town,

The white-faced halls, the glancing rills,
   And catch at every mountain head,
   And o'er the friths that branch and spread
Their sleeping silver through the hills;

And touch with shade the bridal doors,
   With tender gloom the roof, the wall;
   And breaking let the splendour fall
To spangle all the happy shores

By which they rest, and ocean sounds,
   And, star and system rolling past,
   A soul shall draw from out the vast
And strike his being into bounds,

And, moved through life of lower phase,
   Result in man, be born and think,
   And act and love, a closer link
Betwixt us and the crowning race

Of those that, eye to eye, shall look
   On knowledge; under whose command
   Is Earth and Earth's, and in their hand
Is Nature like an open book;

No longer half-akin to brute,
   For all we thought and loved and did,
   And hoped, and suffered, is but seed
Of what in them is flower and fruit;

Whereof the man, that with me trod
   This planet, was a noble type
   Appearing ere the times were ripe,
That friend of mine who lives in God,

That God, which ever lives and loves,
   One God, one law, one element,
   And one far-off divine event,
To which the whole creation moves.

'Come into the garden, Maud'

I

Come into the garden, Maud,
  For the black bat, night, has flown,
Come into the garden, Maud,
  I am here at the gate alone;
And the woodbine spices are wafted abroad,
  And the musk of the rose is blown.

II

For a breeze of morning moves,
  And the planet of Love is on high,
Beginning to faint in the light that she loves
  On a bed of daffodil sky,
To faint in the light of the sun she loves,
  To faint in his light, and to die.

III

All night have the roses heard
  The flute, violin, bassoon;
All night has the casement jessamine stirred
  To the dancers dancing in tune;
Till a silence fell with the waking bird,
  And a hush with the setting moon.

IV

I said to the lily, 'There is but one
  With whom she has heart to be gay.
When will the dancers leave her alone?
  She is weary of dance and play.'

Now half to the setting moon are gone,
    And half to the rising day;
Low on the sand and loud on the stone
    The last wheel echoes away.

V

I said to the rose, 'The brief night goes
    In babble and revel and wine.
O young lord-lover, what sighs are those,
    For one that will never be thine?
But mine, but mine,' so I sware to the rose,
    'For ever and ever, mine.'

VI

And the soul of the rose went into my blood,
    As the music clashed in the hall;
And long by the garden lake I stood,
    For I heard your rivulet fall
From the lake to the meadow and on to the wood,
    Our wood, that is dearer than all;

VII

From the meadow your walks have left so sweet
    That whenever a March-wind sighs
He sets the jewel-print of your feet
    In violets blue as your eyes,
To the woody hollows in which we meet
    And the valleys of Paradise.

VIII

The slender acacia would not shake
   One long milk-bloom on the tree;
The white lake-blossom fell into the lake
   As the pimpernel dozed on the lea;
But the rose was awake all night for your sake,
   Knowing your promise to me;
The lilies and roses were all awake,
   They sighed for the dawn and thee.

IX

Queen rose of the rosebud garden of girls,
   Come hither, the dances are done,
In gloss of satin and glimmer of pearls,
   Queen lily and rose in one;
Shine out, little head, sunning over with curls,
   To the flowers, and be their sun.

X

There has fallen a splendid tear
   From the passion-flower at the gate.
She is coming, my dove, my dear;
   She is coming, my life, my fate;
The red rose cries, 'She is near, she is near;'
   And the white rose weeps, 'She is late;'
The larkspur listens, 'I hear, I hear;'
   And the lily whispers, 'I wait.'

XI

She is coming, my own, my sweet;
    Were it ever so airy a tread,
My heart would hear her and beat,
    Were it earth in an earthy bed;
My dust would hear her and beat,
    Had I lain for a century dead;
Would start and tremble under her feet,
    And blossom in purple and red.

Tithonus

The woods decay, the woods decay and fall,
The vapours weep their burthen to the ground,
Man comes and tills the field and lies beneath,
And after many a summer dies the swan.
Me only cruel immortality
Consumes: I wither slowly in thine arms,
Here at the quiet limit of the world,
A white-haired shadow roaming like a dream
The ever-silent spaces of the East,
Far-folded mists, and gleaming halls of morn.

　Alas! for this gray shadow, once a man –
So glorious in his beauty and thy choice,
Who madest him thy chosen, that he seemed
To his great heart none other than a God!
I asked thee, 'Give me immortality.'
Then didst thou grant mine asking with a smile,
Like wealthy men who care not how they give.
But thy strong Hours indignant worked their wills,
And beat me down and marred and wasted me,
And though they could not end me, left me maimed
To dwell in presence of immortal youth,
Immortal age beside immortal youth,
And all I was, in ashes. Can thy love,
Thy beauty, make amends, though even now,
Close over us, the silver star, thy guide,
Shines in those tremulous eyes that fill with tears
To hear me? Let me go: take back thy gift:
Why should a man desire in any way
To vary from the kindly race of men,
Or pass beyond the goal of ordinance
Where all should pause, as is most meet for all?

A soft air fans the cloud apart; there comes
A glimpse of that dark world where I was born.
Once more the old mysterious glimmer steals
From thy pure brows, and from thy shoulders pure,
And bosom beating with a heart renewed.
Thy cheek begins to redden through the gloom,
Thy sweet eyes brighten slowly close to mine,
Ere yet they blind the stars, and the wild team
Which love thee, yearning for thy yoke, arise,
And shake the darkness from their loosened manes,
And beat the twilight into flakes of fire.

Lo! ever thus thou growest beautiful
In silence, then before thine answer given
Departest, and thy tears are on my cheek.

Why wilt thou ever scare me with thy tears,
And make me tremble lest a saying learnt,
In days far-off, on that dark earth, be true?
'The Gods themselves cannot recall their gifts.'

Ay me! ay me! with what another heart
In days far-off, and with what other eyes
I used to watch – if I be he that watched –
The lucid outline forming round thee; saw
The dim curls kindle into sunny rings;
Changed with thy mystic change, and felt my blood
Glow with the glow that slowly crimsoned all
Thy presence and thy portals, while I lay,
Mouth, forehead, eyelids, growing dewy-warm
With kisses balmier than half-opening buds
Of April, and could hear the lips that kissed
Whispering I knew not what of wild and sweet,
Like that strange song I heard Apollo sing,
While Ilion like a mist rose into towers.

Yet hold me not for ever in thine East:
How can my nature longer mix with thine?
Coldly thy rosy shadows bathe me, cold
Are all thy lights, and cold my wrinkled feet
Upon thy glimmering thresholds, when the steam
Floats up from those dim fields about the homes
Of happy men that have the power to die,
And grassy barrows of the happier dead.
Release me, and restore me to the ground;
Thou seëst all things, thou wilt see my grave:
Thou wilt renew thy beauty morn by morn;
I earth in earth forget these empty courts,
And thee returning on thy silver wheels.

Milton

O mighty-mouthed inventor of harmonies,
O skilled to sing of Time or Eternity,
   God-gifted organ-voice of England,
      Milton, a name to resound for ages;
Whose Titan angels, Gabriel, Abdiel,
Starred from Jehovah's gorgeous armouries,
   Tower, as the deep-domed empyrëan
      Rings to the roar of an angel onset –
Me rather all that bowery loneliness,
The brooks of Eden mazily murmuring,
   And bloom profuse and cedar arches
      Charm, as a wanderer out in ocean,
Where some refulgent sunset of India
Streams o'er a rich ambrosial ocean isle,
   And crimson-hued the stately palm-woods
      Whisper in odorous heights of even.

Epigrams 1868–74

I

What I most am shamed about,
  That I least am blamed about;
What I least am loud about,
  That I most am praised about.

II

Somebody being a nobody,
Thinking to look like a somebody,
Said that he thought me a nobody:
Good little somebody-nobody,
Had you not known me a somebody,
Would you have called me a nobody?

III

What I've come to, you know well,
What I've gone through none can tell.

IV

Gentle Life – what a title! here's a subject
Calls aloud for a gentleman to handle!
Who has handled it? he, the would-be poet,
Friswell, Pisswell – a liar and a twaddler –
Pisswell, Friswell – a clown beyond redemption,
Brutal, personal, infinitely blackguard.

V

Popular, Popular, Unpopular!
'You're no Poet' – the critics cried!
'Why?' said the Poet. 'You're unpopular!'
Then they cried at the turn of the tide –
'You're no Poet!' 'Why?' – 'You're popular!'
Pop-gun, Popular and Unpopular!

Crossing the Bar

Sunset and evening star,
   And one clear call for me!
And may there be no moaning of the bar,
   When I put out to sea,

But such a tide as moving seems asleep,
   Too full for sound and foam,
When that which drew from out the boundless deep
   Turns again home.

Twilight and evening bell,
   And after that the dark!
And may there be no sadness of farewell,
   When I embark;

For tho' from out our bourne of Time and Place
   The flood may bear me far,
I hope to see my Pilot face to face
   When I have crost the bar.

Notes

I have ignored merely uncommon or obsolete words and expressions that the reader can look up for himself in an ordinary dictionary, partly to encourage that healthy habit, partly to save space. But I have tried to explain very rare words, and also uncommon usages of familiar words that might mislead the unwary (e.g., 'conceit' in 'Morte d'Arthur').

Mariana: published 1830. Tennyson said, 'The *moated grange* was no particular grange, but one which rose to the music of Shakespeare's words.' The reference is to the end of act III, scene i of *Measure for Measure*.

    page 24, line 12: marish-mosses – 'the little marsh-moss lumps that float on the surface of water' (Tennyson's note).

Song (*A spirit haunts*): published 1830. An excellent example of a poem of which nothing more can really be said than, 'Look at this. Good, isn't it?'

The Kraken: published 1830. A kraken is a huge (still unidentified) sea monster first mentioned in the eighteenth century as having been seen off Norway.

    page 27, line 13: i.e. when the world comes to an end on the Last Day.

The Lady of Shalott: published 1832. The story is mainly Tennyson's own invention. The nature of the curse is not altogether clear, but presumably the Lady, after an indefinite period of isolation in a dream-world, is destroyed by making a move towards contact with reality in the person of Lancelot.

    page 28, line 10: willows whiten – i.e. they show the light-coloured undersides of their leaves in gusts of wind.

    page 29, line 19: the mirror is part of a tapestry-maker's equipment, to give a view of the right side of the tapestry, as well as being a magical device.

    page 29, line 29: pad – an easy-paced horse used for travelling.

Œnone: published 1832, begun 1830. Œnone was originally an oread, a semi-divine being attending the spirit of a mountain; hence her references here to Mount Ida as her mother. Paris, a prince of nearby Troy, had been her lover, but abandoned her in favour of the wife of the King of Sparta, Helen, with whom he eloped to Troy, thus (later) bringing about the Trojan War. As the poem indicates, he had won her in advance by awarding the prize in a superhuman beauty contest to Aphroditè, goddess of love, in preference to Herè or Pallas (Athenè), goddesses respectively of power (roughly) and wisdom.

page 34, line 10: Gargarus – the peak of Mount Ida.

page 34, line 13: Troas – the land around Troy. Ilion – the city of Troy itself.

page 35, line 21: Simois – a river near Troy.

page 36, line 3: Hesperian – of the Hesperides, a garden where golden apples grew.

page 36, line 4: ambrosially – ambrosia was the food of the gods.

page 36, line 17: Peleus – a Greek king at whose marriage-feast the fatal challenge was issued.

page 36, line 19: Iris – goddess of rainbows, which she used as a high-speed route when acting as the gods' messenger.

page 37, line 8: peacock – Herè's attendant bird and emblem.

page 37, line 18: champaign – a fertile plain.

page 38, line 15–page 39, line 6: lines sometimes taken as suggesting that Tennyson was already trying out his paces as a poet of uplift and morality. However, Paris does not hesitate before accepting Aphroditè's short and to-the-point offer; though, again, this may just help to show how bad he is.

page 38, line 24: sequel of guerdon – 'addition of reward' (Tennyson's note).

page 39, lines 12–13: 'Idalium and Paphos in Cyprus are sacred to Aphroditè' (Tennyson's note).

page 40, line 5: pard – leopard. Homage by wild beasts to human or humaniform beauty is found all over folk-lore and myth.

page 40, line 30: the Abominable, uninvited – Eris, goddess of discord, caused all the trouble just because, alone among the goddesses, she was uninvited.

page 42, line 4: Cassandra – a princess of Troy who had the

gift of prophecy, but with the reservation that her prophecies would never be believed. Here she foresees the fall of Troy to the besieging Greeks.

The Lotos-Eaters: published 1832. In Homer, Odysseus and his men visit the land of the lotos-eaters and partake of the flower or fruit (evidently containing some tranquillizing drug). Tennyson omits Homer's conclusion of the episode, in which Odysseus rounds up his crews and drives them weeping back to their ships.

page 47, line 20: amaranth, moly – vaguely supernatural flowers with some connections with various real amaranths (of which love-lies-bleeding is one) and molies (of which wild garlic is one).

page 48, line 25: the Elysian, or happy, fields were the scene of one of the more optimistic Greek visions of the after-life; equivalent to Paradise.

page 48, line 26: asphodel – a flower whose roots the dead were thought to feed on. The word is etymologically connected with 'daffodil'.

Ulysses: published 1842, but supposedly written in a single day three weeks after Tennyson heard the news of Hallam's death in 1833. (See Introduction.) We are to imagine Ulysses (=Odysseus) after his eventual return to and repossession of his island kingdom of Ithaca, fretting at inaction.

page 50, line 4: unequal – giving some citizens privileges over others. Ithaca was not a democracy.

page 50, line 10: Hyades – stars (real ones) thought to portend rain when they rise with the sun.

page 51, line 33: Happy Isles – another version of Paradise, located somewhere in the Atlantic.

Morte d'Arthur: published 1842, written 1833-4. Tennyson's main source for the Arthurian legends was Malory's *Le Morte Darthur*, printed by Caxton, 1485.

page 53, line 1: the battle at which the Knights of the Round Table were destroyed.

page 53, line 4: Lyonesse – 'the country of legend that lay between Cornwall and the Scilly Islands' (Tennyson's note).

page 53, line 11: on one – it was an idiosyncrasy of Tennyson's to write 'one' where most people would write 'the other'.

page 56, line 17: conceit – irresponsible fancy.

page 61, line 4: 'from which he will some day return – the Isle of the Blest' (Tennyson's note).

Break, break, break: published 1842, probably written 1834.

Will Waterproof's Lyrical Monologue: published 1842, written about 1837. In those days a waterproof would have been a kind of oilskin, but it is curious that a raincoat should even then have been the journalist's uniform. Similarly, the Cock Tavern in Fleet Street was at that time as much a resort of writers as it is today.

page 63, line 8: Lusitania was the Roman province that included what is now Portugal. Will is turning down any 'port-type' concoction.

page 65, line 1: raffs – 'scraps' (Tennyson's note).

page 65, line 16: pipe – not a pipe in the usual sense, but a cask containing upwards of a hundred gallons.

page 66, line 13: George Canning was appointed Premier in 1827, the year of his death. Also a minor poet.

page 67, line 12: taw – 'the game of marbles' (Tennyson's note).

page 69, line 15: ana – anecdotes, letters, reminiscences, etc., connected with authors, as in Shakespeareana, Johnsoniana, etc.

Locksley Hall: published 1842, written 1837–8. Tennyson said he was dealing with 'an imaginary place and an imaginary hero', but there is evidence that he was adapting events in his own life. The 'I' of the poem returns to the scene where he and his cousin Amy fell in love, before, under parental pressure, she jilted him and married another man.

page 79, line 5: the Mahrattas, a people of western India, rose against the British in 1817 and were put down with some bloodshed.

page 80, line 12: Joshua successfully petitioned the Lord to make the sun stand still (which involved the moon standing still 'in (=above?) the valley of Ajalon') so that the Israelites could finish massacring their Amorite enemies.

page 80, line 16: Cathay – ancient China.

Come not, when I am dead: published 1850, written significantly earlier, perhaps about 1838. The 'child' here and the Amy of 'Locksley Hall' are evidently one and the same.

Songs from The Princess: I–IV published 1847, written any time between 1839 and 1847; V–VII published 1850, written 1848–9.

page 83, line 7: underworld – for once, an ambiguity. The main meaning is 'under the horizon', but there is also a sense of 'abode of the dead'.

page 84, line 25: Danaë – a Greek princess imprisoned in a tower into which Zeus, having temporarily turned himself into a shower of gold, made his way with amorous intent. A bold metaphor, and rather odd to find in Tennyson.

page 85, line 18: foxes among vines appear obscurely but destructively in The Song of Solomon, ii, 15, and this is the parallel usually quoted. But Samson, in Judges, xv, 5, less obscurely but also destructively, uses foxes among vines too. A minor puzzle.

page 85, line 19: silver horns – snowy peaks.

page 85, line 31: azure pillars – smoke from cottage fires.

In Memoriam A.H.H.: published 1850, mostly written earlier (see Introduction).

page 89, line 21: him who sings – Goethe, admired by Tennyson.

page 92, line 17: weeds – clothes, especially those of mourning.

page 96, line 10: Phosphor – 'star of dawn' (Tennyson's note). See also page 187, line 9.

page 103, line 17: 'he died at Vienna and was brought to Clevedon [in Somerset] to be buried' (Tennyson's note).

page 107, line 18: Argive – there was nothing specially philosophical about the ancient city of Argos. A synonym for 'classical Greek'.

page 107, line 20: Arcady – the classical home of pastoral poetry.

page 115, line 11: Æonian – age-long, eternal; from 'aeon', as also page 164, line 5.

page 116, line 17: Urania – classically, the Muse of astronomy, but here that of religious poetry.

page 116, line 22: Parnassus – the mountain of the Muses. The first 'thy' has the force of 'thy own part of'. Urania is telling Tennyson to stick to lyric poetry.

page 117, line 1: Melpomene – Muse of song and tragedy.

page 118, lines 2–3: 'The yew, when flowering, in a wind or if struck sends up its pollen like smoke' (Tennyson's note).

page 120, line 15: secular to-be – 'aeons of the future' (Tennyson's note).

page 122, line 2: Lethe was a river of Hades from which dead souls had to drink, upon which they forgot their past lives. The line (rather ineptly) means, 'if death brings oblivion'. See also page 167, line 16.

page 127, lines 11–12: must mean 'the life of Christ', but it is an elaborate, or clumsy, way of putting it.

page 130, line 19: tare – tore.

page 140, line 11: compare note on 'The Lady of Shalott' line 10.

page 145, line 4: hoodman-blind – blind man's buff.

page 145, line 16: in fee – as an absolute and rightful possession.

page 149, lines 3–7: Hallam had been engaged to Tennyson's sister Emily.

page 155, line 9: i.e. at Cambridge, where Hallam and Tennyson first met.

page 156, line 20: 'the broad bar of frontal bone over the eyes of Michael Angelo' (Tennyson's note) also appeared in Hallam's features; supposedly a mark of intellectual power.

page 156, line 22: quicks – quickset hawthorn or whitethorn. See also page 183, line 2.

page 158, lines 23–4: i.e. 'before Venus, the evening star, had dipt into the sunset. The planets, according to Laplace [French astronomer], were evolved from the sun' (Tennyson's note).

page 159, line 4: this bitter seed – i.e. the idea set out in the next stanza.

page 160, line 4: bird – Tennyson said he meant the kingfisher.

page 161, line 17: sightless – invisible, as also in page 183, line 8.

page 162, line 24: fluttering urn – i.e. the flames under the tea-urn.

page 163, line 2: lit – alighted; filmy shapes – i.e. moths.

page 165, line 1: you – probably Emily Sellwood, whom Tennyson married in 1850.

page 165, line 5: one – Hallam.

page 167, line 9: you – some imaginary person, according to Tennyson.

page 167, line 25: gnarr – 'snarl' (Tennyson's note).

page 173, lines 3–4: Anakim – Biblical giants, as Titans are classical giants.

page 179, line 2: rathe – early, immature; a Miltonic use.

page 180, line 24: set light by – 'make light of' (Tennyson's note).

page 183, line 24: crescent prime – 'growing spring' (Tennyson's note).

page 187, line 1: Hesper – Hesperus, the evening star.

page 187, line 21: dearest – Tennyson said, 'If anybody thinks I ever called him "dearest" in his life they are much mistaken, for I never even called him "dear".'

page 188, line 14: paints a bow – 'turns into a miniature rainbow' (Tennyson's note).

page 191, line 12: a general reference to revolutionary violence in Paris.

The final section refers to the marriage of Tennyson's sister Cecilia to his friend Edmund Lushington.

page 195, line 23: the stars shook when Zeus approved Peleus's marriage to Thetis.

Come into the garden, Maud: The long poem, *Maud*, of which this is the best-known part, was published in 1855, mostly written 1854–55, though one passage goes back to 1833–34. The 'I' of the poem is, most of the time, a long way from being Tennyson.

Tithonus: published 1860, mostly written 1833 (see Introduction). Tithonus, a prince of Troy, was beloved by Aurora, or Eos, the dawn-goddess, who offered him one wish. He chose eternal life, not eternal youth, with the results Tennyson alludes to. The setting of the poem is some undefined region in the skies.

page 204, line 30: goal of ordinance – 'appointed limit' (Tennyson's note).

page 205, lines 31–2: Apollo, god of music, created Troy by the power of his song.

Milton: published and written 1863. The metre was invented by the Greek poet Alcaeus about 600 B.C. and adapted into Latin by Horace in the 1st century B.C. Tennyson said he was thinking more of the Greek model. Doubtful.

Epigrams: never published in Tennyson's lifetime; written 1868–74.

page 208, IV: J. H. Friswell, now completely forgotten, had attacked Tennyson and also written a book of essays, *The Gentle Life*.

Crossing the Bar: published and written 1889.

page 210, line 3: an impressive and, as it stands, quite unintelligible line. Philip Hope-Wallace tells me that, in the common estuary of the rivers Taw and Torridge in Barnstaple (or Bideford) Bay, the joining of their waters and the incoming sea can between them, if conditions are just right, produce a loud moaning sound above the sand-bar at the mouth of the inlet. Tennyson almost certainly borrowed the idea from 'The Three Fishers', a poem by Charles Kingsley, who had lived in that part of North Devon. To my knowledge, Tennyson never had, and I suspect he was attracted by the emotional overtones of Kingsley's phrase – 'and the harbour bar be moaning' – without understanding its origin or its reference, we can confidently infer, to a local superstition. Otherwise, why did he, normally a scrupulous self-annotator, leave no note on the line? It certainly needs one.

page 210, line 15: my Pilot – an image that has caused some uneasiness. Tennyson said, 'The Pilot has been on board all the while, but in the dark I have not seen him;' well, yes, but it is when a departing ship has crossed the bar that it *drops* its pilot. Tennyson may have had in mind the older sense of the word, 'one who steers or directs a vessel' (not necessarily in inshore waters), the sense retained in aeronautical use. He could hardly have talked of his Coxs'n, Quartermaster or Navigating Officer, true, though 'Captain' would have done the job quite adequately. But then he might have wanted to avoid reminding his readers of the Captain in Whitman's popular poem.

More about Penguins and Pelicans

Penguinews, which appears every month, contains details of all the new books issued by Penguins as they are published. From time to time it is supplemented by *Penguins in Print,* which is a complete list of all available books published by Penguins. (There are well over three thousand of these.)

A specimen copy of *Penguinews* will be sent to you free on request, and you can become a subscriber for the price of the postage. For a year's issues (including the complete lists) please send 30p if you live in the United Kingdom, or 60p if you live elsewhere. Just write to Dept EP, Penguin Books Ltd, Harmondsworth, Middlesex, enclosing a cheque or postal order, and your name will be added to the mailing list.

Note: *Penguinews* and *Penguins in Print* are not available in the U.S.A. or Canada

KINGSLEY AMIS

Lucky Jim

The hilarious send-up of academic life which helped to set
the style of post-war fiction and placed one of today's most
popular novelists firmly on course for fame.

'*Lucky Jim* deserves all the recognition it has won. It is
highly intelligent and very funny' – C. P. Snow in the
Sunday Times

Take a Girl Like You

The Virgin's Progress of attractive little Jenny Bunn, come
south to teach . . .

'The best novel Mr Amis has written; it has the comic
gusto, the loathing of pretension that made *Lucky Jim* so
engaging and high-spirited' – Elizabeth Jennings in the
Listener

'Incendiary stuff . . . a really formidable blaze. This is his
most *interesting* so far . . . and no less funny than the first' –
Karl Miller in the *Observer*

I Like It Here

Foreigners; Abroad; anything with a hint of garlic and over-
expansive gestures is poison to Garnet Bowen (Swansea
Welsh, ambitious hack academic; a man born to be
exasperated), until his publishers send him to Portugal and
he becomes a literary detective on the trail of the Great Man
who may be a fake. Naturally, Portugal and the Portuguese
are funny and ridiculous; the wife and kids get restless; and
the Great Work he knows he has in him never gets written. But
there are compensations. Abroad may not be so bad after all.

Also available

The Anti-Death League

The Egyptologists (with Robert Conquest)

Not for sale in the U.S.A.

POET TO POET

In the introduction to their personal selections from the work of poets they have admired, the individual editors write as follows:

Crabbe Selected by C. Day Lewis

'As his poetry displays a balance and decorum in its versification, so his moral ideal is a kind of normality to which every civilized being should aspire. This, when one looks at the desperate expedients and experiments of poets (and others) today, is at least refreshing.'

Henryson Selected by Hugh MacDiarmid

'There is now a consensus of judgement that regards Henryson as the greatest of our great makars. Literary historians and other commentators in the bad period of the century preceding the twenties of our own century were wont to group together as the great five: Henryson, Dunbar, Douglas, Lyndsay, and King James I; but in the critical atmosphere prevailing today it is clear that Henryson (who was, with the exception of King James, the youngest of them) is the greatest.'

Herbert Selected by W. H. Auden

'The two English poets, neither of them, perhaps, major poets, whom I would most like to have known well, are William Barnes and George Herbert.

Even if Isaac Walton had never written his life, I think that any reader of his poetry will conclude that George Herbert must have been an exceptionally good man, and exceptionally nice as well.'

Gerard Manley Hopkins

Poems and Prose

Selected and edited by W. H. Gardner

With that boyish gusto which is sometimes found in Hopkins's
letters to his relations and friends, he once remarked to Robert
Bridges: 'What fun if you were a classic!' At that time
Hopkins himself was an unpublished poet with very little
prospect of even getting into print, to say nothing of being
honoured by posterity. Now, however, the slow dialectic of
time has brought in its compensations. Chiefly through the
care and foresight of Bridges, the small but precious collection
of Hopkins's poems has been saved from oblivion. Not only
has this 'eccentric' and 'obscure' Victorian poet-priest
attained the once undreamt of distinction of being widely
read, discussed, and lectured on, but we can now reasonably
assume that he himself has been raised to what might be
called, in his own idiom, that 'higher cleave' of posthumous
being – the status of a classic.

This volume includes four early poems by Hopkins, some
fifty of his best-known poems and several unfinished verses
and fragments, as well as prose extracts from addresses,
diaries and the journal, together with twenty-seven letters to
friends.

Penguin Modern Poets

Representative poems by Kingsley Amis appear in the second
volume of this series, which includes the following:

* Not for sale in the U.S.A.
† Not for sale in the U.S.A. or Canada